I0593247

the
Roller Derby
darling
and the
delinquent

THE BRISBANE BACHELORS SERIES

THE ROLLER DERBY DARLING AND THE DELINQUENT

ISBN: 978-0-6488899-8-4

Copyright © 2022 by Jennie Kew
Published by Wooden Key Press
Proofread by Hot Tree Editing
Cover design by Mayhem Cover Creations

PREVIOUSLY PUBLISHED AS
SACRIFICE AND SEDUCTION (2020)

www.jenniekew.com

sexy, heartwarming, sometimes tear
inducing, slightly kinky joy ride!"
Review for *Third Time Lucky*

"The story is heartwarming and empowering.
The plot is gripping and keeps you turning
pages. Definitely one click worthy."
Review for *Third Time Lucky*

"This novel was so romantic!
I'm in love, love, love with Rafe!
I will read this book again it was so good!"
Review for *This Time Around*

"...Toby was my perfect book boyfriend."
Review for *His Own Heaven*

"It's a sexy, sleek and highly addictive story."
Review for *His Own Heaven*

"Their story is heartfelt, sweet, deliciously
hot and sexy, romantic and more."
Review for *The Viking Blues*

For Nelly and Lissa,
They know why.

I am not what happened to me.
I am what I choose to become.
CARL YUNG

Chapter One

"He's single, you know."

"Huh?" Karen dragged her gaze away from the sexiest man she'd ever had the pleasure to lay eyes on and turned to face her friend. "Did you say something?"

Claire Morse—now Claire Hardcastle—didn't quite roll her eyes. "I said, he's single," she repeated, then nodded in the direction of the man in question. The man standing on the other side of the Italian restaurant, watching the wedding reception with an intense sweeping gaze that made him look more like Luke Hardcastle's bodyguard than his chauffeur.

"Edward? Luke's best man?" Claire continued. "You haven't taken your eyes off him all afternoon."

"Your point?" Karen said with a shrug, hoping she looked more casual than she felt.

"Go talk to him. Ask him to dance."

Karen laughed nervously and shook her head, her long blonde hair fanning around her shoulders as she did. "Yeah, I don't think so."

Claire's gaze softened. "I know you're still dealing with what happened in November, but it's not like you to be shy. What's going on?"

"Nothing," Karen said, throwing her hands up in a gesture of surrender. "I swear."

But Claire wasn't having any of it. "Spill," her friend demanded.

Biting her lip to silence herself would only work for so long, and over the last year, Claire had morphed from Karen's quiet, reserved boss into her dearest friend who brooked no refusal. She wasn't going to let this go, and her pointed stare proved that.

Letting out a sigh, Karen caved. "Fine. November aside, Edward is...." How the hell did she explain this to someone like Claire, someone who'd hit the jackpot on the first go? Someone who'd grown up on the same side of the tracks as her squillionaire husband? "Well, he's... ah, not the type of guy who'd ever date a girl like me. Not seriously, anyway. And usually—previously," she corrected, "I would have been fine with that, but, you know," she half groaned, half pleaded, "it's Edward."

Sexy, funny, cool-as-fuck Edward. A casual fling with a man like him would only end one way: a broken heart. And Karen didn't do casual anymore.

Not going there.

"What do you mean?" her friend asked, her brow scrunched.

And that right there was one of the things she loved most about Claire, and simultaneously hated. The woman had grown up in a bubble—an emotionally and often physically abusive bubble, to be sure, but a bubble nonetheless—and she was still learning how the world really worked. Yep, naïve was Claire's middle name. Most of the time it was adorable. Most of the time it wasn't directed at Karen. "I see you two flirting all the time." She lowered her voice and leaned closer. "Even since November."

Karen cast her a sideways glance and chewed on her lip. "But that's all it is. Flirting. A few harmless quips here and there when he and Luke drop you off and pick you up from work, a wink and a smile and a how-you-doin'?" she said. "He's never there for very long, so we don't talk about anything real. Not *really* real, you know? Flirting doesn't mean anything."

Claire's gaze turned shrewd. The woman might be naïve, but she was also highly observant. "Except it does, doesn't it? It means something to you."

Karen slumped back in her chair and picked at the pale pink sequins on her dress. "But not to him."

And that was the sore point.

"You don't know that," Claire said. "And what do you mean, he's not the type of guy to date someone like you? You have so much in common."

Karen snorted. "Like what?"

"Off the top of my head? Books, music, cars...." Claire counted off on her fingers.

"Just because he's a chauffeur doesn't mean he's into cars," Karen said. When Claire opened her mouth to interrupt, she cut her off and added, "Besides, I'm not *that* into cars."

That time her friend did roll her eyes. "Oh, please. You practically lick the window every time a vintage—" She waved her hand as she sought the right word. "—*whatever* drives past the shop. Besides, you're brilliant. Why wouldn't he want to go out with you?"

Karen bit her lip to hide her pleased smile. "You're my best friend. You're supposed to think that."

"I *am* your best friend, which means I'm supposed to kick your arse when you're being silly. Like right now. I mean, imagine the possibilities if you had an actual conversation with the man instead of just flirting."

"You make it sound so easy."

"It is easy."

"Says the bride on her wedding day."

"Hey, it wasn't all roses and kittens with me and Luke, remember? I admit, I fantasised about him naked on a regular basis—still do, in fact—but I also fantasised about pushing him in front of a bus on more than one occasion."

Karen smirked. "Your point?"

"My point is that it was only after we started *talking* to each other, instead of making assumptions, that we started to connect on a meaningful level. And I think if you tried talking to Teddy—"

"Teddy?" Karen asked, one eyebrow winging up.

"It's what his friends call him, which you would know if you talked to him. And do you know a really good place to talk at a wedding?"

Lips pursed in a moue of resignation, Karen said, "I'm sure you're about to tell me."

"On the dance floor." Claire gave her a nudge. "Go on. Ask him to dance before... *oooh*, too late. Serena beat you to it."

"What?" Karen sat up straight and spun her head in Edward's direction so fast it was a minor miracle she didn't give herself whiplash. Then she gritted her teeth and forced down a growl as she watched the barely legal daughter of their friend and restauranteur, Angie Campioni, sidle up to Edward and bat her thick, luxurious eyelashes at him. "That little—" She let her growl loose. "Well, I'm not going over there now."

Claire snickered. "Oh, come on. It's not his fault he's sexy as fuck."

"Who's sexy as fuck?" Claire's new husband, Luke Hardcastle, sat down beside them and kissed his wife's cheek.

"You are, my love," her friend replied instantly, the broad smile decorating her face doing little to disguise the look of "oh shit" in her wide eyes.

"Nice save." Luke chuckled, then cupped his hand behind Claire's head and pulled her in for a deep and languid kiss.

Karen almost sighed out loud as she watched them. Claire and Luke's road to happily-ever-after had been a bumpy one, what with Claire's aunty trying to destroy Luke, and Luke blackmailing Claire, but everything had turned out all right in the end. As evidenced by the fact they'd said "I do" that afternoon in an intimate ceremony in the botanical gardens and were flying out that night for a month-long honeymoon, touring the south of France and the Mediterranean.

When Luke pulled back from the kiss, Karen smirked at the doe-eyed look on Claire's face. Her friend was the very definition of head over heels in love, but as happy as she was for the couple, she couldn't help the tiny pang of jealousy that stabbed at her heart.

No one had ever looked at Karen like that, like their world began and ended with her. Sometimes she wondered if anyone ever would.

Oh sure, plenty of men looked at her, in a creepy leering sort of way. Many of them were quite vocal about it too, even more so when she failed to show them the gratitude they felt they deserved for pointing out how fuckable she was. Because God forbid she should walk down the street, minding her own business, and *not* have some total wanker call her a bitch, or a slut, or the insult to end all insults, a "fucking Karen".

"Did you ask her yet?"

Luke's deep voice dragged Karen back from her irritable thoughts, and she suddenly found herself the centre of attention as both newlyweds turned to stare at her.

"Ask me what?" she asked slowly, a tingle of caution shooting up her spine.

Claire shared a secretive look with her husband before returning her gaze to Karen. Biting her lip to contain her smile did nothing to lessen the excitement shining in the steel blue of her eyes. "I wanted to talk to you about Novelteas."

"Oh my God." Karen let her head fall back as she groaned. "It's your wedding day, Claire! Can we not talk shop on your wedding day? You know I'm more than capable of running the bookstore for the whole freaking month you'll be away."

Geez. Have a little faith.

Her friend grinned. "I know you're more than capable. That's what I wanted to talk to you about."

Karen had to admit, the look of barely restrained glee on Claire's face had her intrigued. "Okay, I'm listening."

"When the month is up, how would you feel about staying on as store manager full time?"

Karen blinked slowly. "But... you're the manager."

"But what if I wasn't?"

The question sat in the air between them as Karen pondered Claire's meaning. Was she really suggesting what Karen thought she was suggesting? No way was Claire just handing over control of her pride and joy for no reason.

Sliding her gaze from Claire to Luke and back again,

Karen pulled her brow down in confusion. "What am I missing?"

Leaning closer as though she were about to impart some grand secret, Claire whispered, "I'm pregnant."

Karen's jaw dropped, and she blinked hard. "I'm sorry, what?"

"I'm pregnant," Claire said again, her smile serene, "and I was thinking about what that means to me, about what I want for my kids, and how I don't want them raised the way I was, like they're an obstacle or a burden. I don't want them thinking they come second to my job." She took a deep breath. "When the baby comes, I intend to take a full year off work, which means I need someone I trust to look after the business, and there's no one I trust to run Novelteas more than you."

Karen sat back in her chair and stared at her friend for what felt like a full five minutes before her power of speech returned. The fact she only blinked twice during all that time meant it was probably closer to five seconds, but she was so utterly stunned and flattered and completely freaked out by Claire's offer that time had ceased to have any meaning.

"Wow, I don't know what to say." Which was highly unusual because Karen was rarely at a loss for words.

Novelteas, the independent bookstore and tearoom Claire had opened less than a year ago, was fast becoming one of the hottest spots in town, and Karen had been right there with her from day one. She had as much pride in their store as Claire did, and every instinct she owned told her to yell "Yes!" and just figure it all out later. But a tiny kernel of doubt began to sprout near the back of her mind.

Should she do it? *Could* she do it? She was a kick-arse assistant manager and knew without reservation she could run the store for one month and hand it back to Claire in tip-top shape.

Absolutely 100 percent certain.

But taking over indefinitely was an entirely different matter. It involved a lot more responsibility and a lot less goofing around. Even now on days when she was left in charge of the store, she had idiots flick dismissive glances over her before asking to speak to her manager, only to look at her with total dismay when she informed them she *was* the fucking manager.

Okay, so she never said the "fucking" part out loud, but she'd been sorely tempted. Did she really want to deal with that sort of bullshit all day, every day?

With Karen obviously taking too long to offer up an answer, Luke said, "Think of these next few weeks as your trial period." His rich voice pulled her back to the conversation and calmed a little of her inner turmoil. "And Claire will still be working part-time in the shop as you transition over."

"That's right." Claire nodded eagerly. "I won't dump you in the deep end." She rested her hand over her belly, making Karen wonder just how far along her friend really was. Claire was a big woman to begin with, tall and curvy, so she could be several months along before anyone really noticed. "We'll make sure you've got everything you need to succeed before I take maternity leave. And even then, I'm only a phone call away if you get desperate," she added with a wink, knowing Karen would rather die before admitting defeat. "But seriously, I know it's a big change and I'm asking a lot. But you'll get all the same benefits as before, you'll keep any leave you've already accrued, and of course, you'll get a pay raise." Claire grasped Karen's hands. "Say you'll think about it?"

Wrenching one hand free, Karen reached for her champagne, then gulped down the crisp, bubbly liquid, draining the glass completely, giving herself a buzz and a moment to fashion a proper response. She'd be lying if she said she hadn't thought about running the shop. Tweaking a few procedures here and there. And a bigger pay packet was nothing to sneeze at, plus better hours. She had more than a few ideas for the tearoom too....

Was there a downside to this?

And... fuck it. Karen *wanted* the job. She worked hard, she was good at what she did, and maybe it was the champagne talking, but she deserved that promotion.

Slowly lowering the glass to the table, she nodded once. "Okay," she said, then swallowed hard.

"Okay, you'll think about it...?" Claire asked cautiously.

"No," Karen said. "Okay, I'll do it."

Claire clutched her chest and breathed out a sigh of what Karen assumed was relief. "Oh, thank God, because I already had this made for you."

"Had what made?"

Claire slid a tiny parcel wrapped in pink tissue paper towards her. "This."

A grin tugged at Karen's lips, and a laugh bubbled up her throat. She grabbed the parcel off the table, the size and shape giving away the contents of the present before she'd even unwrapped it. And as she peeled back the tissue paper to reveal her new name badge, her laughter exploded out of her. For almost a year, the words *Assistant Book Nerd* had sat beneath her name. But no longer.

From now on, Karen Walker would be known to all as *Da Boss*.

Chapter Two

Edward tried like hell to ignore the riotous laughter coming from the bridal table. But even as he checked the latest weather and traffic reports and calculated the number of minutes required to get the happy couple to the airport on time, he couldn't mistake the exuberance of Karen Walker's laughter. There was a quality about her, a liveliness that lit up the room, and he found himself drawn to her like a moth to a flame.

"So... what do you think?"

"Huh?" Edward was so engrossed in not-quite-ignoring Karen, he'd completely zoned out on the conversation he'd been having with Serena. "About what?"

The teen girl laughed, a deep throaty purr guaranteed to drive all the boys crazy—and, rumour had it, already did. "About helping me buy my first car."

"Why can't your brother help you?"

"Marcos?" Serena rolled her eyes. "Ugh, unless the discussion is about how to make the perfect passata, he's useless. Please, Edward? I've been saving since I was fourteen, and I don't want to get ripped off, you know? And

Mama said I should ask you because you helped her get a good deal on her new delivery van. Come on. Please? You know about this shit."

Edward scowled at the girl. "Language."

"Ugh." Serena rolled her eyes again, reminding Edward of his younger sister, and it struck him that he'd only known the girl—most of the people in the room, in fact—for six short months. And yet he felt like he'd known these people for years. As someone who tended to keep to himself, it was an odd realisation. "Please, Edward," she pleaded, drawing his focus back to her. "Please, please, please, please—"

He held up his hands and surrendered with a laugh. "Okay, I'll help you. Just stop saying please."

"Thanks, Edward! You're awesome."

The girl leaned up and hurriedly kissed his cheek, then ran off towards the kitchen, and he went back to pretending he wasn't watching the pretty blonde he'd been undressing with his eyes all damn day, because *fuck!* Karen was wearing the hell out of that bridesmaid's dress.

He guessed the bride had let her bridesmaids choose their own dresses, seeing as Lottie, Claire's new sister-in-law, and Karen both wore different styles yet in the same shade of pale pink. Both women looked gorgeous, but only one held his attention.

And it wasn't the one making out with her imposing boyfriend in the middle of the dance floor. As cute as Lottie was, she wasn't for him.

Karen was the one he wanted.

The woman he craved.

And her dress was fun, flirty, and short, kinda like her, and covered in sequins that caught the light, then reflected it back. Every time she moved, she shimmered.

Like a beautiful mirage.

A mirage he wanted to see up close and personal, wanted to feel with his own two hands so he could make sure it truly existed. One he could disappear into and slake his thirst.

One he could—*would*—happily drown in.

From the moment they'd met, Edward had been fascinated by Karen. At first glance, he'd assumed the worst about her, had thought her nothing more than an airhead. Gorgeous but ditzy. She was too excitable, too... bouncy. Like a blonde Tigger.

In his experience, bouncy girls were, at best, annoying. At worst, calculating and manipulative. And he hadn't the patience to put up with either option.

On the day they'd met, he'd gone to the bookshop to pick up Claire for a meeting with Luke, only Claire hadn't been there. Karen had offered to help find her, and what had ensued was the weirdest game of phone tag ever between him, Karen, and Luke. In the end, their efforts had proved fruitless.

Claire had eventually shown up at Luke's office building, wondering what all the fuss was about, but for two hours, Edward had waited at Novelteas on Luke's orders, just in case she returned there, so for two hours, he'd watched Karen work... and she'd completely blown his assumptions out of the water.

Edward had never seen someone work so hard, except maybe his father. Karen was a motivated woman, driven and dedicated. And Edward had sat in awe of her. He had no idea how she managed to do all the things she did at once: work the till, answer the phone, recommend books, make sales, make jokes, and direct people to the tearoom upstairs for the afternoon special.

To top it off, she did it all with a smile and an upbeat attitude.

He remembered thinking her cheeks must have ached like a bitch at the end of the day. His face hurt just thinking about smiling that much. Thank God the only person he had to please was Luke, and that man didn't give two shits if Edward smiled or not, as long as he showed up on time and did his job.

Outside of work, however, was a different matter.

Casting his gaze to his boss, he grinned as he remembered the day Luke had asked him to be his best man. The day he'd seen his always cool, calm, and collected mentor fumble for words over beers after work.

"I'm not sure what's sadder," Edward had said with a laugh. "A billionaire with so few friends, he asks his chauffeur to be his best man, or a chauffeur with so few friends, he says yes."

Luke had laughed at that, then said, "You're more than my chauffeur and you know it, you little shit. You're family."

Family.

Edward had worked for Luke Hardcastle for six years and was closer to him than he was to his own father. Not that he saw Luke as a father figure. An older brother, perhaps. Not that either of them ever would have admitted as much before Claire came along and taught them both a thing or two about the true meaning of family.

Especially the kind you made for yourself.

Looking around the restaurant, Edward took in the small but happy crowd. Luke and Claire's found family. The one they'd made together when Luke had embarked on a hare-brained scheme for revenge and bought up all the shops along Merthyr Road—including Claire's bookstore and Angie Campioni's Italian restaurant.

A family that, against all logic, included him—a reformed entitled rich kid who did a six-month stretch for boosting cars, amongst other things.

When his gaze fell on the bridal table again, he caught Karen staring at him, and he couldn't help the way his lips lifted in a lopsided grin as her cheeks turned pink. She did that a lot, he'd observed. Stared at him when she thought he wouldn't notice. Problem was, he *always* noticed, but just like when she flirted with him, he never let it go too far.

He couldn't.

It wasn't that he wasn't interested—the hard-on desperately trying to escape his pants every time he saw her left no doubt about that—but Karen was very... *good*. Not in a goody-two-shoes way—her twisted sense of humour proved Karen was no saint. No, she was good in a community-minded, "always ready to lend a hand", "hard work and a healthy spirit are the path to happiness" way.

As much as he'd turned his life around in the past few years, Edward knew he'd never be a good person, not really, and he'd be damned if he tainted someone as sweet as Karen with his darkness.

At least, that was what he'd like to think. But before he knew what he was doing, he was halfway across the room, his focus zeroed in on the sexy blonde with the bright blue eyes and the killer smile. And that darkness he wanted to shield her from?

Yeah, it had other ideas.

Especially when he saw Marcos get there before him and ask her to dance.

"Fuck," he muttered, arriving about ten seconds too late to intervene.

Marcos winked as he ushered Karen past him. "You snooze, you lose, Berringer."

Edward glared at the smarmy prick but bit his tongue. The last thing he wanted to do was ruin Luke and Claire's evening by starting a fight. He doubted Angie Campioni would appreciate him beating the shit out of her son either, no matter how much Marcos deserved it.

"Is it time to go already?" Luke's question momentarily grabbed Edward's attention away from Karen and her dance partner.

He checked his watch again, then shook his head. "Not quite," he said, folding his arms across his chest. "We have a little time before we have to get you crazy kids to the airport." Then he turned his attention back to the dance floor and continued glaring at Marcos, snarling as he watched the little shit pull Karen close and slide his hands over her hips. "If he touches her arse, I swear I'll fucking punch him."

A muffled chuckling sounded behind him... and that right there was the problem with being friends with your boss.

Luke knew everything there was to know about Edward, including his love life, or his distinct lack of one during the last few months. It hadn't taken Luke long to put two and two together and realise Edward's shift in gears had something to do with Karen, and as good as Luke's skills of observation were, they were nothing compared to his wife's.

Edward glanced over his shoulder to see Claire smirking at him. Yeah. She knew. Edward had a feeling the woman was part mind reader, or maybe a witch. Either way, Mr and Mrs Hardcastle were having way too much fun at his expense.

"Karen can take care of herself," Claire said, a secretive

smile tugging at her mouth. "That said, I'd appreciate you checking in on her while we're away." She frowned. "She has a tendency to overwork and forget to eat."

"Does she?" he murmured. *Interesting.* He let his gaze drift back to Karen. "Did she accept the promotion?"

"Yep."

"And she knows about...." Edward nodded towards Claire's not yet obvious baby bump. The secret only a select few knew about.

"She does."

One side of his mouth twitched up. "How did she react?"

"She went into shock, sculled a glass of champers, then said she'd take the promotion."

"She sculled a glass of champagne?" Edward turned to watch Karen again, scowling when he saw her misstep and press her hands against Marcos's chest. "I didn't think she was a drinker."

"She's not," Luke said, also frowning at Marcos.

Edward grunted. "Okay. I'll keep an eye on her."

A *very* close eye.

Starting now.

Striding out onto the dance floor, Edward tapped Marcos on the shoulder. "May I cut in?"

"No," Marcos said at the exact same time Karen said, "Yes."

Edward smiled broadly but resisted the urge to snap his teeth at the shorter man. "You heard the lady."

Marcos glared at him, and for a moment, Edward didn't think the little brat was going to let Karen go, but then he stepped back and told Karen he'd see her after closing.

Taking Karen firmly in his arms, Edward moved them

across the floor in a slow swaying motion. "What did he mean, he'd see you after closing?"

"Oh, that was nothing," Karen said with a shrug. "He asked me to join him and some other people for a late-night game of Scrabble and a few drinks."

One brow winged up. Edward knew all about Marcos and his late-night Scrabble sessions, and they rarely if ever included other people. He wondered if Karen knew that. "Did he say who else was going to be there? Specifically."

"No one specifically," she said. "Just some of the restaurant staff. Why?"

"No reason," he replied, tugging her closer.

Karen grinned. "You're not jealous, are you?"

"Jealous of what?" Edward snorted. "Playing Scrabble with a twerp like Marcos?"

She pulled back and stared up at him, eyes narrowed. "You really don't like him, do you?"

"It's not that I don't like him, it's just— Yeah, I really don't like him."

Karen laughed, the sound washing over him, cleansing him of his earlier irritation. "Well, if it makes you feel better, I wasn't going to stay anyway. It's already been a really long day, and I'm exhausted. My feet are killing me."

"Shit, why didn't you say something?" Edward brought them to a standstill in the middle of the dance floor. "Do you want to sit down?"

"I'm all right. Unless...," she hedged.

"Unless what?"

"Unless there's a foot rub on the table." Karen smiled sweetly and batted her eyelashes at him in an over-the-top way that made him laugh out loud. No one made him laugh the way she did, or as easily.

Edward grinned down at her. "I suppose you'd like me to carry you back to your seat while I'm at it?"

"It's either that or I get clingy."

Eyebrows shooting into his hairline, Edward needed clarification on that one. "Clingy?"

"Yeah. Oh, but not in a horrible stalkery ex-girlfriend kind of way. I just meant I don't want to fall on my arse in front of everyone. My feet hurt so badly in these shoes I'm amazed I'll still standing."

Glancing down at her fancy footwear, he shook his head. The spiked heel had to be almost five inches high. "Why are you wearing shoes like that anyway? I've never seen you in anything like them before."

"Okay, one, heels in a bookshop are just totally impractical. And two, Claire and Lottie both tower over me, even in flats, and I was attempting to even the odds."

His lips twitched up in a half grin. "And how's that working out for ya?"

She smiled brightly. "Better if I knew there was a foot rub coming."

A chuckle bounced its way through Edward's chest, and he swung her up into his arms, revelling in the feel of her pressed so firmly against his chest. "Fine. I promise I won't let you fall on your arse. Clingy or not."

Chapter Three

Karen wrapped her arms around Edward's neck, enjoying the scent of his musky cologne and the sight of a five o'clock shadow darkening his cheeks, and held on tight as he carried her back to the bridal table. Claire and Luke had vanished, probably saying their final goodbyes before they had to leave for the airport.

Edward set her down on a chair and proceeded to remove her shoes. "How are you getting home tonight?"

It took her longer to answer him than it should have. His hands were so warm, so strong as they unfastened the fiddly little buckles and slipped the strappy stilettos off her feet, and she couldn't stop her mind from forming an image of those same hands slipping her bra straps off her shoulders, unfastening the clasp in back, cupping her breasts in those big, strong hands....

Her cheeks heated, and she had to shake her head to shoo the image away. "Figured I'd order an Uber after the newlyweds take off," she said, finally.

Edward grunted. "Not happening," he said, lifting her feet into his lap.

"I beg your pardon?" Karen protested, then groaned as Edward pressed his thumbs into the arches of her aching feet.

"If you hang around here waiting for an Uber, Marcos will take it as a sign you want to *play Scrabble*," he said in a way that made the board game sound like a euphemism for something far more deviant. Which it was. Marcos was infamous for his triple word score.

"And *playing Scrabble* with Marcos is a bad thing?"

Karen emphasised the same words to tease him, but when he lifted his face to hers, he was scowling, and when he spoke, his voice was dark with warning.

"Marcos is a player, Karen, and inviting women to stay after closing is his standard move. You're better off steering well clear of him."

"It's funny that you think you have to tell me that," she said, smiling at him. Then she leaned forward conspiratorially and added, "Everyone on Merthyr Road knows about Marcos and his fondness for *Scrabble*." She leaned back again. "Besides, I already said I wasn't staying."

"Yeah, but you said you weren't staying because you were tired, not because you weren't interested in playing Scrabble with Marcos."

Edward suddenly went very still, as though he hadn't meant to say what he'd just said. As though he hadn't meant to sound jealous of the guy who hadn't stood a chance in the first place. Not when Karen only had eyes for Edward and had done ever since she'd met him.

Not that Edward knew that.

Yet.

And she was still of two minds about telling him. On the one hand, she wanted him, badly, and knew down to her bones he would rock her world in the sack. On the other hand, it had only been three months since November, since her world had been turned upside down.

Since she'd learned the hard way to be more guarded. Less trusting.

Teasing Edward was the safer course of action, but just as she opened her mouth to say something, his smartwatch vibrated and dinged. "Saved by the bell," she said, grinning at his pained expression.

Pulling his phone from his inside jacket pocket, Edward typed in his passcode and frowned. "Shit," he muttered. "We have to go."

At Edward's serious tone, Karen shifted her feet to the floor and dropped her teasing attitude. "What? Why?"

"There's been an accident on the main route leading to the airport. Looks like they've started detouring traffic through other routes. Fuck. If I want to get Luke and Claire to the airport on time, we have to leave now." He put his phone away, then tugged Karen close enough that their knees touched, and she felt the warmth of his body as he caged her against her chair. "Don't get an Uber. Come with us to the airport, and I'll drive you home afterwards."

"You don't have to do that," she said, her heart suddenly racing at his nearness and the intensity of his gaze. "It's been a long day for you too."

Edward took her hands in his and helped her to her feet, and she tried not to focus on the tingling sensation skating over her skin, heated and electric. *Alive.* "It's no trouble at all. Really. And this way we can send them off together. I think they'd like that, don't you?"

Karen smiled and nodded. He was right. Claire and Luke loved sappy shit like that. "That would actually be pretty great. Okay. Thanks."

"Good. You grab your shoes and purse, and I'll try to find the happy couple. It's go time."

He turned to go, but Karen caught his sleeve. "Hang on a sec. Hunting those two down individually will take time we don't have."

"Agreed. But what choice do we have?"

"Give me a hand."

"What are you—"

Edward frowned at her but held her steady as she climbed up on the table. "There they are, talking to Lottie and Nate," she said, then cupped her hands around her mouth and called, "Oi! Mr and Mrs Hardcastle!"

Luke saw her first, his gaze quickly followed by Claire's, who burst out laughing. "What on Earth are you doing?" she called back.

Karen tapped her wrist to indicate the time. "Change in plans. You have to go. Now." Then she reached down for Edward, gripping his shoulders as he held her waist and lifted her to the floor. "Thank you," she murmured, trying to ignore the heat of Edward's hard body as she slid down his front until her bare feet hit the floor.

"No, thank *you*," Edward said, grinning broadly. Like a man with something to say.

Eyes narrowing, Karen asked, "What?"

He leaned down and whispered in her ear, "The next time you wear a dress that short, I suggest you don't stand on the tables."

"Oh God!" she moaned, squeezing her eyes shut tight as her whole body heated with her embarrassment.

"Nice panties, by the way."

Before her brain could form an appropriate response, Luke and Claire joined them at the bridal table. "What's going on?" Luke asked.

Edward stepped back. He was all business again. "Sorry to rush you both, but there's been an accident. A truck turned over on the main road, and we have to detour around it, so it'll take a little longer to get to the airport. I'm afraid we have to leave now."

"Oh." Claire suddenly seemed flustered. "Angie. I haven't said goodnight to Angie."

"I'll get her," Karen said.

"You wanna go up on the table again?" Edward pressed his lips together as though holding back his laughter, then smoothed out his features into something more serious. "I promise I won't look."

Karen shook her head and chuckled, let go of her embarrassment for the greater good, and climbed back up on the table. "Yes you will."

"Yes. I will."

Karen flagged down Angie, and Claire and Luke said their finals goodnights to everyone. Then she and Edward herded the newlyweds into the back of a vintage Rolls Royce with "Just Married" written on the back window and headed for the airport.

With all the detours they had to take to avoid the accident, and the increase in traffic that slowed everything down to a crawl, it took nearly an hour to drive what should have only taken twenty minutes.

Karen sat in the front of the car with Edward but chatted happily to everyone as they drove. Claire reminded her of a book signing event coming up at Novelteas, and Luke reminded Edward to finalise a business proposal they'd been working on. Karen asked permission to change a few things around in the tearoom, and Edward offered to help out since he'd have more free time than usual.

An involuntary shiver ran up her spine at the thought of

spending more time with Edward. The relationship they currently enjoyed was safe. Flirting—for the brief periods of time they were in each other's presence—was safe. But if those periods of time expanded, it could lead to actual conversations... or more.

The slew of possibilities was terrifying.

He'd seen her panties, for fuck's sake. What if he did want more? What if he didn't? What if Karen put herself out there only to find out Edward had zero interest in her as a potential girlfriend?

After all, why would a man like Edward Berringer—a man from a wealthy, well-connected family—ever want to go out with a bogan from Logan like her?

She was ready to start a new chapter in her life, one that involved commitment and stability and not going to bed alone every night. But better to go it alone than with someone who didn't want the same things she did.

Forcing a smile, Karen said, "I'm sure you'll have better things to do than hang around Novelteas and help with the heavy lifting."

He chuckled, the sound warm and relaxed. "I'm sure I can find time to squeeze you into my not-so-busy schedule."

When Edward pulled into the drop-off zone and killed the engine, they all fell silent. Karen couldn't explain why, but the moment felt... huge. It felt like the end of an era and the beginning of a new one. One she wasn't sure she knew how to navigate and was more than a little freaked out by.

One by one they exited the car. Edward and Luke grabbed the bags out of the boot, and Claire pulled Karen into a hug. "You're going to do great. I know it."

"I wish I had your confidence."

"You have my complete confidence."

Karen poked her friend in the shoulder. "You know what I mean."

Claire stared down at her, a wide smile decorating her pretty face. "I know exactly what you mean. I also know that you know how to do this job blindfolded. You've got this, you'll see. And when you're feeling overwhelmed—"

"I know, I know. You're only a phone call away."

"You call us on our honeymoon, and we'll disown you," Luke growled as he and Edward walked past them, weighted down with luggage as they headed towards the terminal. "Come on, sweetness. We have a plane to catch."

They turned to follow the men inside, and Claire leaned down to whisper, "I was going to say, when you're feeling overwhelmed, fuck Edward."

Karen's shock exploded out of her so fast she almost choked on it. "Excuse me?"

"Sex is a perfectly acceptable way to relieve frustration."

"I know that, but why are *you* telling me that?"

"Because, since losing my V-card, I've discovered sex is a great way to unwind at the end of the day."

Karen's gaze narrowed on her friend. She could always tell when Claire wasn't telling her the whole truth. The woman was a terrible liar. "And...?"

Claire grinned. "And Luke bet me a thousand dollars that the pair of you are too chickenshit to take your flirting to the next level, and I hate losing."

A thousand dollars?

Goddamn rich people.

"Oh, well, in that case, I'll definitely see what I can do," Karen said, sarcasm dripping from her every word. Not that her friend seemed to notice.

"I'd appreciate it."

One last round of goodbyes was shared, and then Karen and Edward left their friends to check in, and Edward drove Karen home.

In near silence.

Awkward, sexually charged silence.

Karen kept sneaking little sideways glances at Edward as they drove through the streets, watching the play of light from the street lamps and restaurants and nightclubs dance across his face.

Edward Berringer was an extraordinarily handsome man. He was tall, but not overly so, and lean but muscled, if what she'd felt under his suit while they'd danced was any indication. His hair was dark and short, and his eyes were a much darker blue than her own. His jaw was strong, his brow regal, and his mouth... a girl could wax lyrical about that mouth.

It was a mouth designed for kissing, for plucking at nipples or tormenting a clit.

Karen breathed out slowly as her brain assaulted her with images of what that mouth could do, and she itched with the urge to reach out and touch him, to slide her hand over his thigh. To feel again the coiled strength she'd felt earlier when he'd pulled her chair close. But when he cleared his throat, she clasped her hands tightly together and held them in her lap.

Until she figured out where he stood on the subject, she'd keep her hands to herself.

"I didn't know you were staying at Claire's old place," he said.

"Uh, yeah, I only recently moved in. I figured it was time I moved to the city, and now that Claire is living with Luke, she needed a tenant she could trust."

He didn't ask any more questions, and silence fell

between them again, just as uncomfortable as before. It weighed Karen down and made her itch with a need to talk, to say anything to fill the void.

Anything to shake the idea Claire had put in her head.

Fuck Edward.

Oh, if only it were that easy. It should have been that easy, and if they'd been in the same situation prior to November, it would have been. Karen would have happily jumped Edward at the bookstore after closing one night, or gone home with him, or hell, even fooled around in the back seat of his car.

If he'd wanted to keep it casual, that would have been fine with her. If it had developed into something more, she would have been good with that too. She'd never given it a great deal of thought before, but she did now.

She had for three months.

She wanted Edward, and physically, she knew he wanted her too. But where did he stand on the rest of it? Had she imagined his jealousy earlier, or was their flirting exactly that and nothing more?

There was one way to feel him out.

"So... Teddy, eh?"

Edward's hands tightened on the steering wheel. "What?"

Karen kept her tone casual. "Claire told me your friends call you Teddy."

He shot her a quick sideways glance, then refocussed his attention on the road. "Some of them do."

"Does Luke?"

"Yes," he said, drawing out the word.

"Does Lottie? Does Angie?"

"Yep." The word came out almost snippy that time, indicating she should probably let the topic drop.

But her curiosity was more than piqued, and she just had to know. Even if it meant hearing something she wouldn't like. "So, why haven't you ever told *me* to call you Teddy?" She twisted in her seat to look at him as he turned the car down her street. "Aren't we friends?"

Edward pulled into the driveway, killed the engine, and heaved a heavy sigh. "Honestly?" he said, a hint of warning in his tone.

Yeah, she wasn't going to like his answer, but she needed to hear it anyway. She needed to know if she was wasting her time going down this path. "Oh, come on," she said with a small laugh, hoping a little levity would lessen the blow she knew was coming. "You've seen my underwear. We have no secrets."

Slowly he turned to look at her, but in the dark interior of the car, she could barely see his face, certainly not enough to read his expression. But she felt his fingertips stroke her cheek and heard the finality in his words. "No, Karen. We aren't friends."

Chapter Four

Karen jerked back, away from Edward and his touch. "Oh."

That was all she said.

One tiny word said with such a tone of acceptance and finality that Edward felt like he was missing something. If Karen had been one of his usual conquests, that "oh" would have been far sultrier, and it would have been followed up with something like "What are we, then, if not friends?"

But Karen wasn't one of Edward's usual conquests, which she demonstrated perfectly by following up her "oh" with "Well, goodnight, then." Then she hopped out of the car with more speed and force than he'd ever thought a woman of her size could possess, and it took a moment for his brain to play catch-up and tell him to go after her.

"Karen, wait. That came out wrong."

Her bare feet thundered up the few wooden steps to the veranda, and a floodlight snapped on, showering them both in a harsh white glow. "Oh, so you didn't just tell me that we're not friends?" she snarled at him as she rifled through her purse, presumably looking for her keys.

Edward reached for her purse. "Let me help."

"Fuck off, Berringer," she snapped, and he couldn't blame her.

Why was it so fucking hard to ask this woman out?

He didn't usually have this problem. Of course, usually all he wanted was a quick fuck, a bit of fun, maybe a repeat or two if the woman was up for it, but something casual he could walk away from if the woman got too close.

The problem was nothing about what he felt for Karen Walker was casual.

"Go for it," Luke had said to him at the airport. "Don't do what I did with Claire. Don't deny how you really feel about her."

Edward had shaken his head and scowled. "She's too good for me."

"We all think that," he'd said, "but here's something no one ever tells you: women think the exact same thing, that we're too good for them. But until one of you gets over yourself and makes the first move, you'll never know."

"You know, sometimes I miss the BC version of you, when you weren't some annoying know-it-all relationship guru."

"BC?"

"Before Claire."

Luke had laughed. "Speaking of the mother of my unborn child, she bet me a thousand dollars you and Karen get together while we're away."

"And did you take the bet?"

"I did," he'd said, barely constraining his glee.

Edward had run his tongue over his teeth, his irritation spiking. "Meaning you think we *won't* get together."

"I do not," Luke had confirmed. "Because I think you're

going to ignore my advice, continue thinking you don't have a shot with her, and completely fuck the whole thing up."

"Your confidence in me is overwhelming," Edward had said drily.

"I'm here to help."

Well, Edward was definitely there to help the smug prick lose a thousand dollars.

Hence him telling Karen they weren't friends and completely fucking the whole thing up.

"Karen," Edward tried again, settling his hand gently over hers. "Let me help."

Looking away from him, she finally relented and let him take her purse. In a matter of moments, he'd found her keys and ushered her inside, shutting the door behind them.

"I'd like you to go, please."

Edward dragged a hand down his face and quietly sighed. He was so damned tired. Too tired to fight this out, and not when Karen was right to be mad at him. "What are you doing tomorrow?" he asked the back of her head, since she was refusing to look at him.

Or maybe she wasn't. Spinning around to face him, her eyes were like bright blue daggers, stabbing into his conscience, and her hands were balled into fists. "Are you fucking serious? You tell me we're not friends and then ask me what I'm doing tomorrow? Really?"

Her burst of anger spurred his own. "Yes, I'm fucking serious. I didn't mean it the way it sounded when I said we weren't friends, and I'd like the chance to explain, but it's almost midnight, I am exhausted, and I still have to drop the Rolls off and then drive home without falling asleep at the wheel."

She stared at him for a moment, then said, "Well, don't let me keep you." Then she held out her hand as if waiting for him to give her something, and he realised he still held her keys and purse. When he didn't hand them over right away, Karen lunged for them, but Edward was taller and faster and lifted his hands over his head where she had no chance of reaching them.

"Give them back," she demanded, leaping for them and missing by a mile.

A grin tugged at Edward's mouth as she tried again and again to snatch back her purse. *She's so fucking cute.* "Not until you tell me what you're doing tomorrow."

She glared at him in a way he'd never experienced from a woman before, and he had to admit he liked it. There was no pretence, no coyness, just fire and honesty and deter-mination.

Breathing hard, she stopped jumping long enough to anchor her hands on her hips and said, "Oh, I don't know. Standing in the backyard and looking for the best place to bury a body sounds like a plan."

"How about I take you out for lunch instead?"

"Why would you want to go out to lunch with someone who isn't your friend?"

Edward chuckled and shook his head. "You're not going to let that go, are you?"

"Why should I?" she snapped.

"Let me take you to lunch and I'll tell you." He handed Karen her belongings. "Please."

She took her things and fiddled with her keys, and Edward could see some of the fight ebbing out of her. She looked as tired as he felt. "Why?"

"So I can apologise properly."

Her gaze flashed with irritation again. "You can do that without taking me to lunch," she said. "I meant why did you say that? That we weren't friends?"

Her words were stained with hurt. He'd done that. He'd hurt her by treating her the same way he'd treated the women of his past, knowing she was nothing like them.

Edward knew there was a mountain of sweet under Karen's shell of sass, and yet he'd mistakenly believed she'd react the same way all those other women had: with an understanding of the game. A realisation that what you saw was not necessarily what you got, that all the little lies they'd told each other to make it to the next level would eventually crumble away and reveal their true natures. Which was usually when they'd part ways and the game would start anew with someone else.

But Karen didn't play games, didn't hide who she truly was. And Edward didn't want anyone else.

Her flirting was artless, her expressions honest. She wasn't some boorish society sophisticate who knew the value of his father's businesses disguised as some random Friday night hook-up looking for a night of fun and free drinks.

She was the woman who occupied every corner of his mind, every second of the day, the woman he could imagine having a life with, a future with. But first he had to convince her he was worth taking a chance on, and that started with fixing the hurt he'd caused her.

Taking a chance, he reached out and stroked her cheek again, relieved when she didn't pull away. "Because we're not," he said gently, then hurried on before she could respond. "Friends don't flirt the way we do, Karen. They don't watch every move you make, especially when they know they shouldn't. They don't fantasise about all the dirty things they want to whisper in your ear when they fuck you all night long." He cupped her cheeks and lowered his face to hers, felt her shallow breathing brush his lips. "And they absolutely don't get a hard-on and want to rip your dress off the instant you climb on a tabletop and flash your panties at them."

"Oh." The tip of her tongue flicked out to moisten her lips. "So, when you say we're not friends...."

"It's because I want so much more from you than that," he growled. "Baby, I am so fucking hard for you right now. How many of your friends have ever said that?"

The sound of keys and a purse hitting the ground was all the warning Edward got before Karen's mouth smashed into his.

Excitement flooded his veins as he deepened the kiss, and his hands tangled in her hair. She was so responsive, so eager, and when he pushed his tongue inside her mouth, she offered no resistance.

When the kiss broke, she moaned his name. "Edward."

A shiver of longing shot up his spine. He wanted to hear that more. That moan. His name. Her voice. Her sweet, sweet voice.

Need gripped him tight. He needed to touch her soft skin, needed to see her perfect little body. Needed to taste her flesh, to lick her pussy and hear her moan again.

"I love the way you say my name." He kissed a path along her jaw. "I can't wait to hear you scream it when I make you come."

He slid his hands down her body, row after row of sequins scratching his palms. He was in no rush, but her dress was so short it took no time at all to reach the bottom, to slip his hands underneath and cup the soft, round warmth of her bare arse.

That was the first thing he'd noticed when she'd climbed up on that table: Karen was wearing a G-string. A pale pink lacy scrap of underwear that did nothing to hide the perfection of her flawless backside. He'd never wanted to bite a woman's arse as much as he had when he'd seen hers.

But even as he nibbled her earlobe and breathed her name, cupped her arse, tugged her closer, and pushed the evidence of his arousal against her soft belly, he knew he had to rein himself in. Knew he had to pull back and take a moment. He couldn't rush this, didn't want to rush her. Edward wanted more than a quick fuck and a bit of fun.

He wanted Karen to be his.

But pulling back was easier said than done when the little minx tightened her grip on his body and moaned, and when she pressed her breasts against his chest and lifted one leg to hook around his, he almost abandoned his plans and let his darkness loose.

"Yes," she murmured against his skin, then ran her tongue up the length of his throat in one agonisingly slow lick before thrusting it back inside his mouth and stealing his breath with another kiss.

Yes. But.... "No," he said, nearly panting with the effort of putting a sliver of space between them. "I want to do this right."

Her hooded gaze and sensual smile were pure seduction. "Your hands on my arse feel right to me," she purred.

Edward leaned his forehead against Karen's and groaned, then squeezed that gorgeous arse again. Fuck, she felt good in his hands. "Woman, you're killing me. Just tell me you'll have lunch with me tomorrow."

She flicked open the top button of his shirt. "Or you could stay the night and join me for breakfast instead." She flicked another button open.

"I can't." He swallowed hard. "There are things you don't know about me. Things I need to tell you before we go too far. Besides," he said, taking a step back, "I have a standing engagement on Sunday mornings. Breakfast with my family. Not showing up is not an option." Not after all the work he'd put into rebuilding those bridges.

In answer to that, she gripped his shoulders and leapt on him, wrapping her legs around his hips. The action forced her dress to bunch up around her waist, and Edward couldn't help the groan that escaped him, the groan that matched Karen's as she ground her lace-covered pussy against his cock. "You sure about that, tiger?"

He cocked one brow. "Tiger?"

"Since Teddy is off the table, because, you know...."

"We're not friends," he finished with a grin.

"Exactly," she said, then attacked his mouth again, waging war on his good sense and crushing his resolve to go slow.

But....

Putting Karen back on her feet, he ended the kiss and smiled down at her. He guessed she was only about five feet and maybe four inches tall. Definitely shorter than his own six feet and one. But she'd taken him by surprise when she'd jumped on him. The woman was certainly nimble, and he wondered if nimble translated to flexible and why the fuck was his brain even going down that path when he was trying *not* to pin her down to the nearest flat service and fuck his way into her?

Taking a breath, he tried again. "Okay. I can live with tiger. But for the love of all that is holy, will you please just have lunch with me tomorrow?"

Karen straightened her dress, then stared at him for what felt like an extraordinarily long beat of time, as though she was trying to figure out what he was up to. As though she didn't trust his motives, which was fair. He hadn't earned that yet. "Okay," she eventually said. "Lunch. Tomorrow."

Edward released a relieved breath. "Do you like seafood?"

"Love it," she said, her eyes brightening again.

"Good. How about I pick you up around ten thirty, and we can drive up the coast?"

"Sounds like a plan."

He grinned. "A better plan than burying a body in the backyard?"

Karen let her gaze travel the full length of Edward's body and back again, then winked and said, "I guess we'll see."

Chapter Five

Edward pulled into his parents' driveway and braced himself for his weekly dose of guilt and disappointment. The only thing making the morning more bearable than usual was knowing he was going to see Karen afterwards.

Karen who'd kissed him like a nymphomaniac and climbed him like a tree.

He smiled at the memory. *Fuck*. It had taken everything in his power to walk away from her the night before. And not skipping breakfast in favour of driving directly to her place that morning had been just as hard.

He had it for her bad.

Which was crazy considering how little he actually knew about her. Besides the fact that Karen was gorgeous, driven, smart, liked seafood, and wore sexy underwear, he knew nothing at all. He hadn't even known she'd moved into Claire's old place. Or where she'd moved from. Or who helped her move in.

So much to learn.

"Teddy, there you are." Edward's sister, Emily, waved from the front door. "You coming inside?"

A few minutes later, he was in their parents' kitchen, surrounded by the sounds and smells of his childhood, sizzling bacon, and freshly brewed coffee. His mother, Elaine, stood at the epicentre of the large chef's kitchen, working the stove and issuing orders while his sister hurried to fulfil them. Their younger brother was nowhere to be seen.

"Can I do anything to help, Mum?"

"Oh, Teddy, sweetheart." She tilted her face towards him and smiled happily when he pressed a kiss against her smooth cheek. "We're just about finished actually, but can you set the table for me, please?"

Edward made his way through to the adjoining room and set out a place setting for each of them, glad to be away from the bustle of activity in the kitchen. The buffet at the end of the formal dining room was already full of food.

His mouth watered at the smell of fried sausages and buttered toast, various fresh fruits, yoghurt and whipped cream, and his father's absolute favourite thing to eat: pear and walnut brioche pudding. Because God forbid David Berringer should eat plain old regular bread and butter pudding like everybody else.

To be fair, his mother's cooking was fucking amazing, and the pudding was delicious.

"Son."

Edward stiffened. *Speak of the devil.*

"Morning, Dad," he said, extending his hand. When his father took it and gave it a firm shake, he breathed a little easier.

Their relationship had always been a difficult one. As

much as Edward loved and respected his father, he resented him a little bit too, and that resentment sat heavily in his chest, making it hard to breathe. But at least they were on speaking terms now. For several years they'd actively avoided each other, until his mother had put her foot down and instigated the Sunday breakfast protocol, making attendance mandatory. She'd forced them to interact, to be civil, and it was for Elaine's benefit only that they held their steady truce.

Emily and Elaine entered the room and placed the last of the food on the buffet. "Where's Easton?"

His dad grumbled something about him being in his room, so Edward volunteered to fetch him.

He bounded up the stairs, taking them two at a time, knocked on his brother's door, then entered. "Hey, Easton, come on. Breakfast is ready." Then the smell of tobacco hit him like a truck. "What the— Are you crazy?"

His teenaged brother ripped off his headphones and swore. "Shit. I thought you were Dad."

"What in the actual fuck, Easton? What the hell do you think you're doing?"

Easton rolled his eyes. "Yeah, like you're one to judge. It's not like I'm stealing cars over here."

Edward's jaw clenched at the jibe, and he reminded himself that his brother was only seventeen and still in the clutches of his lizard-brain phase of life. Common sense and responsibility were not high on his list of priorities.

At twenty-eight, Edward knew better. He'd already made his mistakes—more than his fair share—and was still paying for the consequences of his actions.

Reaching out, he snatched the lit cigarette from Easton's hand and dropped the disgusting thing in the half-full mug of coffee on the desk.

"Hey! I was drinking that."

"Come downstairs and get a fresh cup," Edward barked at him. "And open the window. It stinks in here."

"That would be the incense," Easton said, throwing attitude at him.

Edward smiled grimly. "No, mate. That would be you kidding yourself. Now open the bloody window and come downstairs." Then he turned to leave, but not before taking pity on the little shit and offering one last piece of brotherly advice. "And change your clothes and brush your teeth. If you're *extremely* lucky, Mum and Dad won't mention the smell." Because his brother was delusional if he thought they wouldn't notice it.

As soon as he re-entered the dining room, Edward grabbed a plate. He didn't fill it as high as he usually would have, which his mother noticed right away.

"Not hungry, sweetheart?"

"Saving room for lunch," he said, spooning marmalade onto his sausages. It was an odd habit of his grandfather's, something he'd picked up whenever he'd visited the old man as a kid. The rest of his family thought it was weird, but Edward liked it.

"Where are you going for lunch?"

Edward was surprised that the question came from his father. Most of their Sunday conversations consisted of his mother peppering her children with questions while his father listened and ate in near silence, only opening his mouth to throw out the occasional opinion or lecture, depending on the subject at hand and which child was involved.

"North coast," he replied. "I have a date."

The D-word made both of his parents sit a little straighter in their chairs. It made his siblings make stupid wooing noises.

"Do we know this one?" his mother asked, her voice a mixture of curiosity and caution.

Edward had brought home some... *interesting* women in the past. Enough to earn his mother's current reaction. Mostly he'd latched on to anyone he thought would annoy his father, forgetting at the time that they'd also be meeting his mother, and she had definitely deserved better from her eldest son.

Karen was 100 percent better.

"Ah, no, you don't. But her name is Karen and—"

Easton burst out laughing as he took his seat. "Karen? Seriously? You're dating a chick named Karen? Did she wanna see your manager?"

Instead of telling him off, Edward sniffed the air and frowned. "Does anyone else smell that? What is that?"

Easton immediately shut up and glared at him from across the table, and his father's eyes narrowed as he stared at his youngest child. Yep. He smelled it. But before his father could deliver a lecture on the evils of smoking, his mother continued the conversation.

"And what does Karen do for a living?"

"She works at Novelteas," he said. "Actually, she's just been promoted to store manager."

"A career girl," his mum said, obvious approval in her voice. "I like it. Where are you taking her?"

"Mooloolaba. I thought we'd eat prawns fresh from the market, then go for a walk on the beach, maybe visit the aquarium if she's up for it."

"That sounds like the perfect first date, doesn't it, babe?"

Edward always got a kick out of the fact that his mum called his dad "babe". She also had a habit of grabbing the man's arse whenever he was in reach and thought her children couldn't see. His father seemed resigned to his fate with a quiet acceptance and a knowing smile, and while he often came across as the antithesis of his happy-go-lucky wife, Edward knew the man would do anything for his wife.

In fact, Edward had always seen his parents' marriage as the ultimate relationship goal and knew without a doubt that he wanted what they had.

A true partnership.

His eagerness to see Karen grew.

"Yes it does," his father agreed with a decisive nod, drawing Edward's attention back to the topic of *his* love life.

"I'm glad you think so," Edward hedged, glancing sideways at his dad, "because I'd like to borrow Betty, if that's okay."

Pausing with a forkful of brioche pudding halfway to his mouth, his dad gave him his full attention. "You want to borrow Betty for a *first* date?" He shook his head. "Betty is more of a closer, son. Not an opening statement."

"Oh, you should take Audrey," his mother said excitedly.

"Excellent suggestion, Elly," David said, his gaze softening as he smiled at his wife. Then to Edward, "Take Audrey. She's the perfect car for a first date."

"I swear I'm adopted," his sister muttered from beside him. "This family is so weird."

"I still can't believe her name is really Karen," his brother added.

"I can't believe Dad names all of his cars after movie stars."

Edward looked at his sister. "I can't believe you haven't named your car at all. *That's* weird."

"And I can't believe you're all letting your breakfast get cold."

A chorus of "Sorry, Mum" echoed around the table.

When the conversation picked up again, Edward was once again surprised it came from his dad. "I expect you'll have some free time on your hands now, what with Hardcastle gallivanting around Europe. I could use someone with your experience at the dealership. No one sells cars like a driver can."

Sighing softly, Edward tried his best to hide his irritation. Of course his father assumed he'd have nothing better to do for the next month than flog BMWs to elitist twats. "Luke isn't gallivanting around Europe, Dad, he's on his honeymoon. And he hasn't left me empty-handed by any stretch of the imagination. I have a list a mile long of everything he wants finalised by the time he returns. Don't worry, he's keeping me busy."

David Berringer raised one dubious, greying brow. "You drive the man's car for a living, son. What could you possibly be doing while he's out of the country?"

Edward had been dreading this conversation. Going to work for his father—as had been expected of him his entire life—had never been a part of his plans. And his refusal to do what was expected of him had been a thorn in his father's paw for almost as long.

Carefully laying aside his knife and fork before he met his father's gaze, he said, "If you must know, I'm putting together a business proposal for Luke. If he likes what he sees, he's agreed to back me financially, be my silent partner, as it were."

His father's gaze narrowed slightly, and Edward may have imagined it, but he thought he saw a begrudging hint of respect shining in one far-flung corner of those old blue eyes. "And what is this business you're proposing?"

"A vintage auto repair shop," he said, straightening in

his seat. "Possibly rentals too, for weddings and functions and such. I'm still researching public liability and insurance, but it's definitely something to think seriously about. Luke paid five hundred dollars to hire a '77 Silver Wraith for the day. Some companies charge that much by the hour, more if you need a chauffeur."

"And the garage side of the operation? How will you secure that side of the business?"

"By filling the void already being created."

"Explain." His father turned in his chair and faced him completely, watched him shrewdly, and Edward knew he was talking to David, the businessman, not his father.

He had to make this good.

"All the old-timers who specialise in vintage cars are retiring, and no one is stepping up to take their place. Older garages are simply shutting down, and their expertise is being lost. My garage would be one of only a handful of specialists in the greater Brisbane region, and vintage cars are always in vogue."

"A lack of competition doesn't guarantee success. What's your advertising strategy?"

"David, do we really need to discuss this right now?" Elaine's voice held a tone of warning, and Emily and Easton bowed their heads over their plates and sighed deeply, bracing themselves for the oncoming storm.

Holding up his hand to silence his wife, David Berringer never took his gaze off Edward. "Yes we do. I want to know how my son intends to support himself. I want to know how a university dropout and ex-con who's done nothing more than drive a rich man around for the past six years thinks he knows how to run a business."

"It's all right, Mum," Edward said, glancing at his mother. He'd known these questions, this day, would come soon enough, so he lifted his chin and stared unflinchingly at his father. "My advertising will consist of a permanent online presence in the form of a dedicated website and social media accounts, plus advertising on online car sales platforms, virtual car magazines, and in traditional print media. Then there's the various annual car shows and swap meets, most of which I'm already well known at and have a respected reputation at, despite my past. Some might even say because of it."

When his father's only response was to run his tongue over his teeth, Edward's frustration flowed out of him like blood from a wound. "How many cars have we rebuilt over the years, eh? How many makes and models? I know vintage cars like I know how to breathe, and I know I can fill that void, fulfil the need for specialist mechanics. Hell, you've had me helping you in the shed since I was old enough to pick up a fucking spanner."

"Edward! Language."

"Sorry, Mum." He took a breath. "Dad, you've taught me everything I know about cars, and Luke's taught me everything I know about business. And I may be an ex-con, but I'm no uni dropout. Not anymore." Edward gritted his teeth as he admitted something he should have told them long ago. "I completed my business degree last year. With honours. I can do this, Dad. I will do this."

David bowed his head for a moment, then nodded and stood. "Okay," he said quietly, then pushed in his chair and left the room.

Edward stared at his half-eaten eggs, poked them with his fork. "Why is he like that?"

Elaine tossed her napkin on the table. "Emily, Easton, can you get started on cleaning the kitchen please?"

"But I'm still eating," Easton complained.

"You'll survive, I'm sure," their mother said drily. "Of course, if you really need something to tide you over, you could always smoke another cigarette."

Edward swallowed down a bark of laughter at the horrified look on Easton's face.

Emily wasn't as kind. "Busted!" she cried, then followed their younger brother as he stomped from the room, muttering under his breath as he went.

Once they were gone, his mother relocated to the chair beside his. "Why didn't you tell him you finished your degree?"

"I honestly wasn't sure he'd care."

She sighed and shook her head. "You two are both so bloody stubborn," she said. "Of course he cares. You're his son. Oh, I know he doesn't always show it, but your father loves you. He just... he worries about you. He always has."

"Not always."

His mother scowled at him in a way she rarely did, an expression designed to put him in his place. "Yes. Always. Do you think it was easy for him, for either of us, watching our son go to prison?"

"Do you think it was easy for me going to prison?" Edward clenched his jaw against the tears he felt stinging the backs of his eyes. He needed to move around, to use the agitated energy he felt coursing through his body. Pushing out of his chair, he began stacking the dishes on the table and took a steadying breath. "We all did what we had to. I know that." He took another breath. "So, what is he worried about this time?"

"That you'll struggle," she said. "The way we struggled when we were starting out. And now you're talking about this Karen girl with that look in your eye—"

"What look?"

This time when his mother shook her head, it was accompanied by a tinkling laugh. "You know exactly what look. This girl means something to you, and your father can see it as plainly as I can. And if he comes on a little harsh, it's because he wants you to do well, wants you to live up to your potential. And I think, maybe, he's also a little hurt you didn't come to *him* with your business proposal."

Edward met his mother's gaze but didn't say anything. What *could* he say to that?

She threw him another knowing look. "It's a very good idea, Teddy. I think a vintage garage sounds like the perfect venture for you." She smiled. "You've always had an affinity for anything mechanical. Even when you were little you were always pulling things apart to figure out how they worked." She rose to her feet and smoothed her hands over his shoulders. "Now, you and Audrey should get going. You don't want to be late. First impressions matter."

"Thanks, Mum." He kissed her cheek and turned to leave but paused by the door. "And hey, tell Dad I can work in the dealership one or two days a week, if he really needs me to."

"I'll tell him. And good luck!"

"Thanks."

He was going to need it.

Chapter Six

When Edward pulled into her driveway, Karen almost swallowed her tongue. He was driving the prettiest powder-blue Datsun Fairlady roadster she'd ever seen in her life. Honestly, it looked showroom new.

And when her date opened the car door and strode across the yard like he owned the joint, she bit her lip so damn hard she almost made it bleed.

Dressed in blue jeans and a black T-shirt, Sketchers, and a pair of Wayfarer sunglasses, Edward looked like the quintessential 1960s bad boy. It was the first time she'd ever seen him out of a suit and tie, and *goddamn*, he looked good.

When his mouth hooked up in one corner, forming a sly grin, she couldn't help but return his sexy smile with one of her own.

"Right on time," she said. "I like a man who's punctual." When he stopped in front of where she stood on her front steps, she added, "Looking good, tiger."

His grin broadened, and Karen tried desperately not to

blush as he looked her over from head to toe. "Thanks. You too."

She frowned slightly and turned from side to side. "I'm not underdressed? I wasn't sure where we were going but figured, you know, Sunshine Coast. Beach-bum chic is always in style up there."

She'd tried on five different outfits in the last two hours before settling on what she was wearing: denim cut-offs, a pale pink tank top with a loose white overshirt, sandals, and togs instead of underwear. It was modest without being dowdy but showed off just enough skin to capture Edward's appreciative gaze.

"You look great," he reassured her. "Definitely not underdressed for what I had in mind. Although...."

Karen froze as uncertainty gripped her lungs and squeezed. "What?"

Edward's grin was swift and cocky. "Please tell me you're wearing a bikini under there."

Biting her lip to stifle a grin of her own, she said very seriously, "I'm wearing a bikini under here."

Her date groaned. "You're killing me, baby."

"You asked," she said, shrugging.

"Yeah, I did." He leaned in and pressed his lips against hers in a surprisingly gentle kiss. "Let's get out of here before I toss you over my shoulder, carry you back inside, and do bad things to you."

A sly smile tipped up her mouth, and she waggled her eyebrows. "What sort of bad things?"

Edward shook his head and chuckled, then held out his hand. "Come on."

Karen took his hand and let him lead her to the car. She appreciated him opening the door for her and the way he held her hand as she seated herself in the low-slung vehicle.

Her dad had raised her to be a strong and independent woman, capable of opening doors all by herself, but sometimes it was nice to let someone else be in charge, to know they could be the strong one and take the reins for a bit. To let someone take care of *her* instead of the other way around for a change.

Besides, the last thing she wanted was to start their date off by falling awkwardly into the seat and making a fool of herself.

Again.

Once she was seated, she pulled her hair up into a messy bun and slid on a pair of aviators. It was a beautiful morning, perfect for driving, and when Edward turned the key in the ignition and she heard that engine purr, Karen knew it was going to be a great day.

Smoothing her palms over the console, door panel, and seat, she marvelled at the quality of the restoration work.

It was exquisite.

"Does she have a name?" she asked as they drove north.

"Audrey," Edward replied, his voice raised so she could hear him over the wind.

"As in Hepburn?"

He grinned. "That's the one."

A Fairlady named Audrey. It was the perfect name for the little car.

Karen laughed. "I love it."

"Wait until you meet Betty," Edward said, winking, then turned his full attention to the road.

Holding a conversation in a convertible was never the easiest thing in the world, and the rest of the drive fell into a companionable silence. Unfortunately, the highway provided no real distractions, with little more to look at than service centres and pine forests lining either side, so her attention fell back on Edward.

The way he held himself as he drove told her he was very comfortable behind the wheel, but she supposed since he drove a car for a living, that was to be expected. She itched to ask him a dozen questions—did he have any siblings? Why did he become a chauffeur? Was his dick as big as she thought it was?—but until they got where they were going, there was no point starting a new conversation. Not unless she wanted to yell herself hoarse fighting to be heard over the wind swirling through the car.

She could reach over and discover the answer to her dick question before they got to where they were going, then thought better of it. She'd never forgive herself if her curiosity caused a car accident.

Eventually, Edward steered the car off the highway, taking the Mooloolaba turnoff. Karen grinned. So that's why he wanted to know if she was wearing a bikini. They *were* headed to the beach. Not that it would have mattered either way. The Sunshine Coast was so laid back, no one cared what you wore as long as you had appropriate footwear.

Her excitement ratcheted up another notch when he parked the car outside the aquarium, and she couldn't help the little squeeing sound that escaped her.

"Please tell me what we're doing today," she said, turning to face him in their seats.

Edward stretched his arm across the back of her seat and turned to face her too, then dropped another of those soft, fleeting kisses on her mouth. "I thought we could grab some prawns from the fish market and find a quiet corner of the park to eat them. Then we could go for a walk along the beach, maybe up to the rock wall and back." He nodded at the aquarium entrance. "Or we could take a stroll under the sea. We have all afternoon and can do whatever you want."

Karen nibbled her bottom lip as she considered their options. Usually after a big night out, she would have slept in for as long as possible, then done as little as possible, only leaving the house in search of the absolute essentials, like a Maccas run, or tampons. She should have been tired after the wedding and the reception, but she'd woken up choc-a-block full of energy to burn.

Boundless, nervous energy.

And since Edward was apparently attempting to be a gentleman by not jumping straight into bed with her, a good feed and a long walk would definitely help dissipate that energy.

"Do we have time to do all of it?"

He checked his watch. "Yeah, I think we could squeeze it all in, as long as we don't linger in any one place for too long."

No lingering meant they'd keep moving, and if they kept moving, it would be so much easier to hide her nerves from him. "Groovy. Let's do this!"

But as they strolled along the Parade, commenting occasionally about the weather or the people or the shops they passed, Karen realised she wasn't the only nervous one. In a burst of... she wasn't sure what—hope or stupidity, depending on the outcome—she grabbed Edward's hand and threaded her fingers through his.

At his shocked expression, she realised stupidity had won the day, and she tried to pull her hand back. When Edward gently squeezed her hand, smiled down at her, and refused to let her go, hope flared back to life and smacked stupidity up the backside of its head, and Karen breathed a little easier.

"I'm glad you said you like seafood," Edward said as they entered the fish market. "I'd have been really disappointed if you'd gone the other way."

Karen assumed her best expression of pearl-clutching horror. "What Queenslander doesn't like seafood?" She dropped her hand. "And I'd have been more than just disappointed if you didn't like it."

He cocked one brow. "Oh? What would you have done?"

She shrugged. "I would have purged you from my life completely and forgotten you'd ever existed."

Edward seemed to mull that over for a moment, then nodded slowly. "Harsh but fair." And then he bought a kilo of prawns and a crayfish to share, and she paid for their drinks.

"You seem to know your way around pretty well," Karen said as they crossed the street to the park and headed for the only available picnic table. "Do you come up here often?"

He separated the prawns into two equal piles, and she immediately dug in, shelling the tasty morsel and shoving it in her mouth in record time.

"I used to," he said, peeling his own crustacean much more slowly and setting it aside. "When I was little. Before they passed, my mum's parents lived up here, and I spent a lot of time with my granddad, building sandcastles and fishing." He peeled another prawn but didn't eat that one either. "What about you?"

"Grandparents or Sunshine Coast?"

He added another peeled prawn to his pile. *Damn*, he was fast. "Either. Both."

Karen watched him, fascinated by his behaviour as she answered. "Never knew my grandparents. They all died before I was born." She shoved another prawn in her mouth. "But my dad used to bring me and my brothers up here once a year. It was always during the winter holidays, so the water was too cold for swimming, but that didn't stop us from trying," she said with a laugh, remembering her brothers daring each other to see how long they could stand in the freezing water before running back to the beach.

"Why always in winter?" Edward asked.

She shifted uncomfortably and focused her attention on peeling her next prawn, a small frown tugging at her brow. "During the off season was the only time Dad could afford the room rates."

Picking up on her discomfort, her date thankfully changed the subject. "How many brothers do you have?"

"Three," she groaned. "I'm the second youngest of the four of us. Eric and Dane are older, and Tim is younger. What about you?"

"I'm the eldest of three. My sister, Emily, is twenty, and my brother, Easton, is seventeen, so there's a bit of an age gap between them and me."

Eyes wide with amusement, Karen said, "Edward, Emily, and Easton?"

"Yep," he replied, his lips quirked into a rueful smirk. "And my mother is Elaine."

"What about your dad?" she asked, eager for the answer.

"David."

"Well, that's disappointing," she said, her shoulders drooping at the unexciting answer. Then she frowned again and pointed at Edward's stockpile of peeled prawns. "Are you going to eat those?"

He grinned. "Yep. I'm a peel first, eat later kind of guy. But I see you're a peel 'em and eat 'em girl," he said, nodding at her diminished pile of prawns. She only had two left.

In response to his cheeky observation, Karen picked up the crayfish, ripped its head clean off, and pointed it squarely at him. "One thing you need to know about me is I don't muck around when it comes to seafood."

The man's expression changed from smug to sexy in the blink of an eye. "That was hot."

She met his gaze and swallowed hard. The man was looking at her like she was next on the menu, and she'd be lying if she said that didn't make her heat up in all the right places.

Pity she couldn't do anything about it.

After lunch, they headed farther down the beach towards the rock wall, fingers entwined between them, shoes dangling from their free hands, toes sinking into the wet sand as the cool water lapped at their feet. As first dates went, this one was quickly racking up as the best one Karen had ever been on.

Glancing up at Edward, she said, "I'm glad you asked me out. I really wanted you to but never thought you would."

"Why not?"

Embarrassment flooded her cheeks with colour, and she ducked her head to hide them. "I don't know. I guess because I grew up poor and you didn't, I figured you'd never be interested in someone like me," she said, then snorted. "Not as girlfriend material anyway. Rich kids were always quick to invite us poor kids to their private parties for a bit of fun, but they didn't dare take us out in public. The idea was laughable to them." Her lips twisted into a grimace. "I guess I was scared you saw me the same way. Fun to flirt with and fuck but not much else."

When he didn't say anything, she chanced to look up at him again and found him staring at her, frowning. "How did you know my family is wealthy?"

He sounded annoyed, accusatory, which only served to bring out her own irritation.

How dumb did he think she was?

"Everything about you screams money," she said, pulling her hand away and folding her arms across her chest, creating a barrier between them. "The way you talk is a dead giveaway, always so proper, even when you try not to be. And then there's the way you walk, the way you hold yourself. Shit, even the way you eat and drink says upper crust."

"And you gleaned all that from our daily flirting sessions at Novelteas, eh?" He still sounded off.

But Karen just rolled her eyes now. "See? Right there. How many people do you know who use the word 'gleaned' in everyday conversation? Not many, if I had to guess. And paying attention to people, *gleaning* information from their habits and mannerisms is what I do. It's what makes me so good at my job."

She huffed out a breath to signal the end of her rant.

Edward moved closer and held out his hand, obviously expecting her to take it. When she didn't move, he sighed. "Do you want me to take you home?"

"No, I want you to tell me why me knowing your family has money made you cross."

"I'm not—"

"Bullshit."

He shook his head, then relented. "Fine. I'm annoyed. But not at you." Edward dropped his shoes and flopped down onto the sand beside them, then pulled his legs up and rested his forearms on his knees. "I'm *cross*," he said, emphasising her word choice instead of his, "because I've been conditioned to be suspicious of women who talk about money, to question their motives." He scrubbed his hand through his short, dark hair. "It's a knee-jerk response, and I hate it."

Karen flopped down beside him and wrapped her arms around her knees. "What do you mean by 'conditioned'?"

It sounded tortuous.

"I mean I've dated enough women over the years who made it very clear they viewed me as their ticket to a better life. And I know that's not you, baby," he added quickly, "but...."

"Conditioning." Yeah, Karen knew what he was saying. She understood. Because she'd been conditioned to expect certain treatment from people in her life too.

Like rich kids only wanting her as a plaything.

"Truthfully though, I was also pissed off you thought I'd only want you for sex." He turned his head to look at her. "I meant what I said last night, Karen. You mean so much more to me than that."

"You hardly know me," she whispered.

"I know enough to know I want to know more. I want to know everything about you, Karen Walker." He turned to face her fully, took her hands in his. "And I need you to know I'm not just here for the sex. I want a relationship, a proper, grown-up, 'introduce you to my parents' relationship."

No one had ever said *that* to her before.

Her gaze locked with his, searched for the lie. Found none. Karen was twenty-six years old, and not once in all that time had anyone ever wanted her to meet their parents.

Shit. Edward was serious.

He wanted a serious relationship.

With her.

Her heart beat so fast she wasn't sure if it was panic or excitement or an unholy combination of the two as she stared at his face, his handsome, earnest face with his dark blue eyes and sinful lips and—

Edward's deep voice interrupted her thoughts. "But if you're not on the same page, just tell me—"

Slamming her mouth against his, she silenced his doubts. And her own. Here he was, Edward Berringer, offering her everything she'd ever dreamed about on a silver platter, and she'd be a fool not to grab it while she could.

Firm hands gripped her shoulders and eased her away from him. "So...?"

Karen laughed. "Yes, we're on the same page. Same chapter, same book—hell, I'm hoping there's an entire series with a massive story arc and plots twists and—"

"And a happily ever after?" he asked, his sexy grin spreading wide.

She nodded, then said, "Is this crazy? Are we crazy? It feels crazy."

Edward laughed and hauled Karen onto his lap, shifting them so they looked out at the water. "It's completely insane, but it's also why I want to go slow, why I didn't want to have sex with you last night."

"That's a relief," she said, grinning even though she knew he couldn't see her face. "I was beginning to think maybe you had an STI or something."

"What?" He laughed again. "How the fuck did you come to that conclusion?"

"No one's ever turned me down for sex before."

His arms tightened around her. "So obviously I must have a sexually transmitted infection."

"Well, we both know it's not because your equipment

doesn't work." She could feel said equipment rising to the challenge as they spoke and wiggled her butt against the thick length of his erection.

A very masculine growl sounded quietly by her ear. "You're going to be trouble, aren't you, baby?"

Turning her head, she brushed her lips over his again. Softly, teasingly. "Don't worry, tiger. You'll get used to it."

Chapter Seven

E dward held Karen's hand all afternoon.

He'd never felt so happy doing something so simple and revelled in the feel of her soft skin pressed against his, the heat of her palm as it moulded to his. The trust she placed in him, allowing him to touch her in a way that let everyone around them know she was his girl.

He held her hand as they walked along the rock wall and back, he toyed with her delicate fingers as they strolled along the beach, and his ego puffed up with male pride when she squeezed his fingers and pulled him closer, stealing kisses as they slowly meandered through the aquarium, watching the sharks circle overhead as the smaller fish scurried out of their way.

And they talked.

About so many things, about books and music and cars. Edward liked knowing his girl was as much of a rev-head as he was. He never would have picked her for it if she hadn't told him. She'd always seemed so much more refined, but it turned out they had much more in common than he'd ever dreamed of. Their love of horror fiction, their aversion to boy bands, and the fact that they both grew up learning the ins and outs of engines from their dads.

He also had to laugh when she admitted she didn't think cars would be his thing either, that it was just his job and not his passion. He took great delight in divesting her of her misconceptions, and she practically salivated at the thought of seeing his father's car collection.

A collection he'd helped his father to painstakingly restore.

He did not, however, tell her about his stint in prison. He would tell her, and soon—she had a right to know—but it wasn't something he could just casually drop into the conversation as they walked through the aquarium. What would he even say? "Oh, and by the way, baby, eight years ago, I did something amazingly stupid and went to prison for six months. Did you know male sharks have two dicks?"

When they got back to the car, ready to leave for the day, Karen said, "Tell me more about Audrey." She ran her hand along the old girl's rear fender.

"What would you like to know?"

Edward put the roof up for the drive home so they could talk more easily, then popped the passenger door open and helped Karen into the car. As soon as he jumped into the driver seat, she peppered him with questions. He answered them all, even told her stories about the restoration, including the time he got stuck in the car, without his phone, because of a faulty seat belt clip, and how he'd been too terrified of what his father would do to him if he dared to cut the strap to escape.

"Five hours I sat there, waiting for Dad to get home. And do you know what he did?"

"What?"

"After five minutes of failing to get the clip to release, he cut the fucking strap! Then he told me off for not thinking of that myself."

Karen's laughter filled the tiny car, and Edward's cock twitched in his jeans as she laid her hand on his leg. But when she slowly inched it higher, when her fingers pressed harder against his inner thigh and nudged his balls, he grabbed her hand and slid it lower.

Away from the danger zone.

His concentration was barely holding on by a thread as it was without Karen touching his dick.

"Behave," he growled, his voice deepened by his raging lust. A lust he had to keep chained.

For now.

If she was still interested after he'd told her everything, then all bets were off.

And by bets, he meant pants.

When they arrived back at her place, he walked her to her door. Karen tried again to entice him inside, and again his cock had risen to the challenge, but he wouldn't be dissuaded from his path. As much as it pained him to not sink into the wet heat of her sweet pussy, he knew the long-term rewards far outweighed the short-term gains.

"When will I see you again?" Karen murmured, her voice breathy as Edward teased her with butterfly kisses across her cheek and down her throat.

"Tomorrow," he whispered against her neck, his own breathing ragged. "Absolutely. I'll pick you up after work and take you to dinner." He nibbled her earlobe. "We can celebrate your first day as manager. And talk some more. There are things you need to know about me."

Karen whimpered, the sound hitting Edward right in

his balls. How the fuck did he think he was going to survive not taking this sexy-as-fuck woman to bed any time soon? But glutton for punishment that he apparently was, he let her go and stepped back, revealing her hooded gaze and slightly parted lips. *Fuck.*

Beating a hasty retreat, he reminded her, "Tomorrow, baby. Five o'clock." And then he jumped back in Audrey, adjusted his aching cock, and got the hell out of there.

Before his resolve crumbled and he let his dick take the lead.

———————

The following day was exhausting, mentally and physically, and the only thing making Edward put one foot in front of the other was knowing he'd see Karen again soon.

He'd been taught about the Goldilocks zone in business school, but one thing he hadn't been taught was how utterly depressing it was trying to find the right premises for a new business.

It couldn't be too small, or he'd never fit in all the equipment and workspaces he needed, and it couldn't be too big, or he'd never be able to afford the rent. But finding something within his price range, that fit his size and power requirements, and in an area of town that wasn't so obscure or remote his future customers would never find him, was easier said than done. Throw in the fact that nearly everybody required him to agree to a background check and he had a feeling he was never going to find a place.

By the time he arrived at Novelteas to collect Karen for dinner, the last thing he wanted to see was a cop car sitting out front.

Edward slammed his way into the shop, panic gripping his lungs like a vice. "Karen? Baby? Where are you?"

A policeman about Edward's height and build stepped out of the office at the rear of the bookstore, his expression foreboding, his chin lifted, and his eyes narrowed. "This him?" he drawled.

Another cop appeared from the stacks to his left. "Yeah, I reckon that's him."

A cold sweat trickled down Edward's spine. Why the hell were the police looking for him? He hadn't done anything wrong, had kept to the straight and narrow—for the most part—for eight years.

I haven't done anything wrong.

"Where's Karen?" he demanded. "Is she all right?"

"We'll ask the questions, thanks," Copper One said, stepping around a book display as he moved closer to where Edward stood.

"Listen," he said, hands held up in front of him, palms open so they could see he wasn't armed. Blood thundered in his ears, narrowing his focus. His body went into survival mode, recognising the threat before him and blocking out everything else. "I don't know what you think I've done, but I guarantee you have the wrong bloke." The two coppers looked at each other but said nothing. Edward swallowed hard. "I promise this is just a misunderstanding."

"No shit," one of them murmured.

"I've kept my nose clean ever since I got out."

The cops stopped advancing on him and shared a knowing look.

"Got out of where?" Karen said, appearing beside him.

Shit. How long had she been there? What had she heard? It didn't matter. These two cops were not on the level, and he had to protect her from them. He grabbed her wrist and dragged her behind him.

"Stay behind me, baby," he said quietly. "Are you okay?"

"Of course I'm okay," she replied, and he heard the confusion in her voice, felt her try to move out in the open. But he blocked her escape, never once taking his eyes off the cops. Edward had learned a long time ago to always keep his eye on his enemy. "Edward, are *you* okay?"

"Aw, look at that," Copper Two said, grinning. "He's trying to protect her."

"Look, whatever you think I've done, just leave her out of it, okay? She's a good person." He tried to back her towards the front door, tried to get her out of there. "Do whatever you want to me, but don't hurt her."

Behind him, Karen huffed loudly, the sound one of impatience. "Will someone please tell me what the bloody hell is going on?"

Copper One narrowed his eyes, tilted his head slightly and folded his thick arms over his chest. "I think we need to ask your boyfriend that one, eh?"

Karen shoved at Edward's shoulder, then ducked under his arm, escaping the wall of protection he'd tried to erect around her. "Don't be a dick, Eric." She pointed at the other one. "That goes double for you, Dane."

Wait. Eric? Dane? Were these arseholes Karen's brothers? Edward's anxiety morphed into anger. He'd thought Karen was in trouble. Because of him. Were these fuck-knuckles just messing with him? Playing a prank on their sister's new boyfriend?

"Your brothers are coppers?" he growled, tense for an entirely different reason as he continued staring at the fuckers in uniform.

"What was your first clue?" Dane said, still grinning like the cat that caught the bloody canary.

Edward lifted his chin but kept his expression blank to hide his seething anger. "Well, it was either that or strippers."

Karen shuddered. "Now there's an image I didn't need in my head." Then she turned back to him and slid her arms around his waist. "And you didn't answer my question. Got out of where?"

Eric laughed and rubbed his hands together. "Oh, this should be good."

Another annoyed sound erupted from Karen. "Out, the pair of you. Stop wasting taxpayer dollars and get back to work, or I'll call the commissioner and dob you in for being layabouts."

The sight of such a tiny woman bossing around two police officers who could easily subdue her if they wished should have made Edward laugh. She looked like a chihuahua chasing a pair of bulldogs as she tried to shoo them out of the bookstore. But he couldn't deny that the anxiety they'd stirred up with their stupid prank had left him feeling even more wrung out than running around in circles all day looking for a workshop.

"Hey," Dane complained as Karen shoved him towards the door, "we only wanted to congratulate our little sister on her promotion."

"That's right," Eric chimed in. "Sizing up the ex-con who thinks he's good enough to date you was just a bonus."

Fuuuck.

Edward glared at the Walker brothers and their stupid smug faces, knowing they'd dumped him in the shit with their sister. *Arseholes.* He couldn't fault them for wanting to protect her, but they obviously didn't consider him that much of a threat if they were willing to leave her alone with him, which only reinforced his opinion that they were arseholes.

He waited until she shut the door before he spoke. "Karen—"

She held up a hand to silence him, pinching the bridge of her nose with the other. "Eric called you an ex-con."

"Ex being the operative term," Edward said quietly.

"But con as in convict. A criminal." It wasn't a question but a statement of fact, one she spat at him accusingly.

"This wasn't how I intended to tell you."

"*Did* you intend to tell me?" she snapped, her voice growing louder even as it shook.

Edward stepped forwards, wanted to hold her hand and reassure her, but she flinched away from him. Afraid of him. "Yes, I did. I was going to tell you after dinner tonight. Hell, I'll tell you everything you want to know right now if you'll let me."

Karen paused for a moment, anguish etched across her lovely face, her hand still on the door handle. She didn't meet his gaze. "Did you... *kill* anyone?"

"God, no. Nothing like that. I did six months in a minimum-security facility. It was like a day spa for white-collar criminals."

She stared at him again, her jaw clenched, obviously still weighing her decision, then turned towards the door.

Edward feared she was going to bolt, that she wouldn't hear him out, but as he followed her gaze, he saw her brothers still standing on the footpath, both of them with their phones pressed to their ears as they watched their sister and the ex-con through the window.

Karen waited, staring at her brothers until one of them gave her a slow thumbs up. Then she flicked the OPEN sign over to CLOSED and turned the deadbolt. The clicking sound it made as it snapped into place was ominous.

But it was the resigned sigh that followed that cracked open his heart.

Chapter Eight

"Let's take this upstairs," Karen said, heading for the stairwell without looking to see if Edward was following her.

She made it all the way to the top of the stairs before she heard the bottom step squeak under his weight. Then she listened to each and every creak of the old timber as he slowly climbed higher.

Finally, he reached the top, but then he just stood there, looking lost, defeated, and so very different from the man she'd come to know.

"You sit there," she said, her voice strung tight as she pointed to one of the tables.

Edward pulled out a chair and sat down, then rested his hands flat on the table, fingers splayed.

Like a prisoner would.

When she sat at a neighbouring table, his jaw clenched, and his beautiful mouth flattened, but he nodded with one short, sharp movement.

"Okay. Whatever you need."

Silence sat heavily between them, awkward and

uncomfortable, just like it had in the car after the wedding reception.

Only this time it wasn't wrought with sexual tension.

Unsure how to broach the topic at hand, Karen simply stared at him. So many questions swirled through her mind. Okay, so he didn't kill anyone. What did he do? Why did he do it? And if it wasn't that bad, why did he hide it from her? They'd known each other for five months. How had this not come up before now?

Did Luke know?

Did Claire know?

Argh! She was going to kill them for keeping this from her. And then she was going to kill her brothers for being dickheads.

Karen was pissed off. If there was one thing she really loathed, it was being lied to. And a lie of omission was just as bad in her eyes.

"This is ridiculous," Edward said, breaking the deadlock. "May I sit with you, please?" When she hesitated, he added, "Your brothers might be arseholes, but I'm pretty sure they wouldn't have left you alone with me if they thought I was going to hurt you."

"Maybe not," she snapped, her anger giving her courage. "But I can't think straight with you so close to me. It's hard enough as it is with me here and you there, so no, you can't sit with me." She breathed deep to calm herself, then met and held Edward's steady gaze. "What you can do is tell me why you were in prison."

He stared at her, silent for so long she began to think he wasn't going to answer her. Then he said, "Unlawful possession of a motor vehicle and destruction of property. I stole a car and crashed it on purpose."

Karen frowned. "Why?"

"Which part?"

"Both?"

Edward smiled, but it wasn't a happy expression. "Basically, I was an entitled rich kid with daddy issues. Clichéd, I know, but there it is."

"You're going to have to give me more to work with than that, please," Karen said and folded her arms across her chest. "Rich kids don't go to jail for crashing a car." Her father had grumbled about the unfairness of the system her whole life. She knew rich kids got away with shit poor kids never would.

Edward exhaled slowly, as if bracing himself for something harrowing, then looked at her again, his eyes painfully sad. "You're not going to like what I tell you, and then you're not going to look at me the same way."

She raised one brow. "And how do I look at you?"

"Like someone worthy of your time. Like a man who's worthy of you." His throat bobbed as he swallowed. "I don't want you to stop looking at me like that."

Karen's lips parted slightly, the shock of his words testing her courage. She didn't want to stop looking at him like that either, but she had to know what type of man he was. She had to know what he'd done.

"Then be that man. Tell me the truth, and trust me to make up my own mind."

"Okay. But if it helps, maybe you could think of this as one of those plot twists you were talking about yesterday." Then Edward scrubbed a hand across his mouth, making his agitation obvious even before he spoke again. "I was at university, studying business and drowning under the weight of my father's expectations." He tilted his head, stared at her curiously. "Did you go to uni?"

"Yes. I studied literature and creative writing."

"And did you enjoy life as a uni student?"

Against her better judgement, Karen smiled. "For the most part. I had a part-time job at the local supermarket, so I had to learn to juggle school and work, but yeah, I think I did all right."

"Did you have friends, a boyfriend? Did you go out?"

"Well, yes." She frowned. "Didn't you?"

"No. When I wasn't studying, I was working at Dad's car dealership. And if I wasn't there, I was at home babysitting my sister and brother, helping them with their homework so Mum could have a break."

"You didn't go out with your friends?"

He scoffed. "Funny thing about friends at that age, if you tell them 'no' often enough, they just stop inviting you. Same goes for girlfriends. When you're never around, they quickly find someone who is."

"So, what did you do to relax, to blow off steam? Everyone needs an outlet, or they'd go crazy."

"Trust me. I know." Edward's gaze narrowed curiously. "Out of interest, how do *you* blow off steam?"

Karen shrugged. "Roller derby."

His eyes widened, but his body went very still. "Fishnets and shorty-shorts roller derby?"

"Uh-huh," she said, biting back a smile at the sound of his interest. This was so not the time to be flirting. She was mad at him and she wanted answers. "But don't change the subject."

"Give me a sec. I'm still imaging your sexy arse in shorty-shorts and roller skates." His smouldering gaze slid over Karen from top to toe, and she shivered, but she had to move the conversation forwards. Get them back on track. Resting her hands on the table, she tapped her fingers impatiently until Edward relented and sighed heavily. "I did nothing to relax. I didn't have time. I didn't make time." His brow pinched in a look of frustration, of irritation. "Until I met a woman named Amber, who introduced me to the world of joyriding."

Karen sat back in her chair and folded her arms across her chest. "Joyriding? Is that what you were doing when you crashed?"

Edward tilted his head from side to side, seeming to think about his answer. "Yes and no." He paused again. "I met Amber at the dealership. She was sexy and sophisticated and knew everything there was to know about the latest models we were selling. She was catnip for a guy like me." He huffed out a scornful laugh. "What I didn't know was that she was a car thief. A member of an organisation that targeted and recruited dumb kids like me to help them."

"Why you, do you think? Besides the fact that you had access to high-end cars."

"Simple. I was angry and lonely. But mostly because I was angry."

"At...?"

"My father. I was killing myself for him, for his dream of a father-and-son team. I had no friends, no girlfriend, no life... and no one to talk to about any of it. And when I tried talking to my dad, he dismissed my concerns out of hand, as though they were beneath his notice. As though *I* was beneath his notice." He shook his head. "Joyriding offered me an escape, a way to get out of my own head for a little while. And it was fun and harmless and such a rush... until it wasn't."

"What happened?"

"One of Amber's crew had photos of me stealing the cars we went joyriding in. She was never in focus, but I sure as fuck was. Clear as day. They threatened to go to the police, to show them proof I was the car thief, unless I helped them knock over my dad's dealership."

"Shit." Karen slumped in her chair, her jaw lax, her mind spinning. "How old were you?"

"I was nineteen."

She frowned. "You were so young. Just a kid."

"Old enough to know what I was doing. Old enough to know better." Edward shook his head, that frustrated brow marring his handsome features again. "It was so stupid! So pointless, reckless. I almost cost my family everything they'd worked for. And for what? Some pussy and a joyride?"

Karen placed her hands on the table and twisted her fingers together. The urge to go to him, to hold and comfort him was so strong, but she needed to hear the whole of it. Needed to know everything he'd done before deciding their fate. Deciding whether or not to trust him with her own secrets.

"What happened next?"

"I refused to help them, said I didn't care if they turned me in. All I'd done was nick a few cars, drive them around the block, and put them back exactly where I'd found them. It was a slap on the wrist at most. At which point Amber told me they'd gone back and stolen each of the cars I'd gone joyriding in."

"Which would earn you more than a slap on the wrist," Karen guessed.

"Up to seven years in prison," he said. "But I still told them no. I didn't care what they did to me, and eventually they figured that out. Then they threatened the one thing I'd do anything to protect."

"Your family."

"Yes." Edward let out a harsh breath and shoved his

hands through his hair. "Suffice to say they painted a vivid and horrifying picture of what they'd do if I didn't cooperate, of what would happen to my mother and sister while my father and brother watched."

Karen's hand flew to her mouth, and tears stung her eyes as her imagination filled in the blanks. Not even her imagination but her memories.

She wanted to vomit. "Jesus."

"So I did what they wanted," Edward said, his voice flat, defeated. "I disabled the security and let them in, I helped them take what they wanted, and then...." An evil grin slowly spread across his face, and he lifted his gaze to hers, showed her the darkness she'd only seen glimpses of until then. "Then I took them on the joyride of their fucking lives."

Chapter Nine

Edward hated remembering that night, hated every fucking detail of everything that had led to him doing what he'd done. He'd been a selfish, immature arsehole. But he was an arsehole who knew the streets of Brisbane like the back of his hand and could drive the shit out of any car they put in front of him. And the car they'd put in front of him that night had just so happened to be designed specifically for what he'd had in mind.

Driving really, really fast.

His grin grew feral as he recalled what he'd done. "There were five in Amber's crew, including her, and I don't know where she found them, but they were dumb. I mean, they were complete morons. None of them noticed when I disabled the security that all I'd actually done was switch the alarm over to silent, that I hadn't disabled it at all. And none of them thought to take different routes to the rendezvous point so they wouldn't all get caught together. And then Amber decided she wanted me in the lead car with her."

One of Karen's eyebrows shot up, and she folded her

arms across her chest again. "Oh?" Her hint of jealousy was fucking adorable and his cock twitched against his thigh.

"Don't worry. This story has a happy...*ish* ending." When she relaxed her arms, he continued. "She wanted to keep an eye on me, I guess. That and she couldn't drive for shit. Anyway, I made sure to drive as recklessly as possible to catch the attention of the police, and it didn't take long for them to catch up to us." He snorted as he recalled the utter stupidity of Amber's crew. "Amber had told her guys to follow me at all costs, so instead of going off on their own when the cops showed up, lights flashing, sirens blaring, they stuck to me like glue. As the lead car, I used that fact to my advantage and led them up Milton Road."

He shrugged. "Traffic accidents are common enough along there." Especially in the older sections where the road narrowed and was often bordered by retaining walls, and road repairs were few and far between. "And at the speeds we were doing, it didn't take much to pretend to lose control of the car and crash. Two of the other cars crashed trying to avoid hitting us, which created a bottleneck too narrow for the others to escape through. Then the cops boxed them in behind us. It was all over in less than half an hour."

In a flash of movement, Karen shot out of her chair at the neighbouring table and slapped her hand against his shoulder. "You could have been hurt!" Another slap. "You could have died!"

Edward grabbed Karen around the waist and pulled her down into his lap, pinned her arms to her sides so she couldn't hit him again, and realised she was crying. Her body shook as she sobbed, and she offered no resistance when he gently pressed her head to his shoulder and stroked her hair, offered her comfort. It comforted him too, holding her like that, snuggled against his chest.

"But I wasn't, and I didn't." She started struggling, but he tightened his grip on her, wrapped his arms completely around her, and held her close. "It's okay, baby. I'm okay."

Karen felt so small in his arms, so warm and soft. Edward knew he'd happily hold her like that all night if she let him. Lifting one hand, he stroked her hair away from her face and softly kissed her furrowed brow. Her bottom lip was pinched between her teeth, and worry permeated her very being, but when she burrowed against him and pressed her face into the crook of his neck, he couldn't help feeling happy. She was worried for him over something that happened more than eight years ago.

She cared about him.

"You don't still drive like that, do you?" she muttered against his neck.

"No, I don't. Not for a long time. Although...." A bark of laughter escaped him. "Funny story...."

"What?" Her tone was cautious.

"Well, when I was released, I found very few people were willing to give a job to an ex-con, so I took what I could get, bounced from job to job for over a year. I did everything from washing cars and scrubbing toilets to stacking shelves at the supermarket." He sighed. "After about eighteen months of that, I was ready to call it quits and beg my dad for a job, any job. But one day I was walking by a restaurant in the city, and I saw this fancy-looking gentleman step out of his shiny new car, and the devil on my shoulder whispered in my ear, 'Why not?'"

"Tell me you didn't?" Karen groaned.

Edward grinned. "I did. I slipped into the driver seat and lit out of there before the valet even stepped off the footpath. And my God, she was a beautiful machine. Sleek black exterior, all leather interior, more mod-cons than you could poke a stick at, and all powered by the sexiest V8 engine you'd ever heard. She handled like a dream, and for the first time in almost two years, I felt alive. Of course, all I did was take her around the block, but still, I'd expected the police to be waiting for me when I got back."

"They weren't?"

"Nope. Instead, the bloke who owned her was standing on the footpath, screaming into his phone about his car being stolen. Have you ever seen a man crush a mobile phone in his hand?"

Her eyes widened, big and round. "No."

"Well, that's what this guy did, right before he punched me in the face." Edward rubbed his jaw as he remembered. "Felt like I'd been hit with a ton of bricks. But what happened next shocked me more."

"Oh?"

"Yeah, he offered me a job. Said if I was so desperate to drive his car, I could meet him at Hardcastle Tower at eight o'clock the following morning."

"It was Luke's car?"

"Uh-huh." Edward smiled. "I had no idea if he was serious or not, but the next day, I was at HQ by half past seven in my best suit and tie. Sonofabitch showed up an hour late, then flipped me off. I've worked for him ever since."

"But why did Luke give you a job? You stole his car."

"Apparently he was impressed by how efficiently I'd gotten through the peak hour traffic in such a short amount of time. That and the fact that I returned the car without a scratch on it."

Karen smiled for a moment, then lowered her gaze and fiddled with Edward's tie pin. He saw the action for what it was: a precursor to an awkward question.

"Why didn't you work for your dad? When you first got out, I mean."

Edward's mood sobered, and he shifted in his seat. Talking about his father always made him uncomfortable. "Our relationship was strained before I went away, and being locked up for six months did nothing to improve the situation. It was too soon for him, the betrayal too fresh in Dad's mind."

"But you stopped Amber's crew from getting away, stopped them from hurting your family."

"And cost my family half a million dollars in lost revenue when I did. Besides, if it hadn't been for me, they never would have been in danger in the first place."

Karen harrumphed. "If your dad had listened to you when you went to him, you wouldn't've been so angry, or so easy for Amber to manipulate."

Edward frowned and pulled back to see her face more clearly. Her tone of voice, that underlying hint of anger, spoke volumes.

And then she stared unashamedly back at him and confirmed his hunch. "I have some experience with being manipulated for someone else's gain."

"You want to talk about it?"

She settled her head on his shoulder. "One sob story at a time, eh?"

After dropping another kiss on her forehead, he continued. "When Dad tried to claim the insurance on the cars I'd wrecked, he hit a wall. Because of my involvement, the insurance company ruled the theft as an inside job and refused to pay up. They actually insinuated Dad planned the whole thing just for the insurance money." He scoffed. "Anyone who knows my father knows how insane that sounds. But while Dad may be a rich man, he wasn't always. He didn't have the connections or influential friendships that come with old money, no way to get around the insurance company's red tape. Certainly no way to keep me out of prison."

"But it was your first offence. You shouldn't have gone to prison at all."

Edward tilted Karen's chin up so he could look her in her eyes. "I stole cars, destroyed property worth hundreds of thousands of dollars, and was incredibly fucking lucky no one got killed in the process."

"But—"

"You come from a family of cops, baby. You know as well as I do, it doesn't matter why I did it," he said. "I broke the law."

He held her gaze until she nodded, until he knew she understood, then let her settle against him once more. "So, what did your father do about the insurance?"

"He didn't do anything."

"What?"

Edward shrugged. "There was nothing he could do. But I could. I cut a deal with the prosecutors. I'd plead guilty, do however much time they deemed fit, and give them every scrap of information I could about Amber and her boys— which was a lot more than they had—in exchange for them proving my father had nothing to do with the theft and helping him cut through the red tape bullshit."

"And they went for that?"

"I'd helped them catch the daughter of the leader of a notorious car theft ring, which in turn led to further arrests. They were happy to oblige. In the end they offered me a reduced sentence and promised me, in writing, that they'd do everything in their power to help Dad."

"And did they?"

"Yes. The evidence they provided was irrefutable. The insurance company had no choice but to pay what was owed."

"Still, it can't have been easy, going to prison," she said, her fingers drawing lazy circles on his chest. "You were only nineteen."

"It wasn't too bad. I mean, it wasn't all sunshine and daises either, but like I said earlier, I served my time in a minimum-security centre south of Brisbane. It could have been a lot worse." He rubbed his hand up and down Karen's back. "And honestly, I think if I hadn't done my time, the guilt of what I did to my family, to my dad, would have crushed me by now."

"But it's okay now? With your dad? This happened years ago, right, so it must be okay by now?"

"We're getting there. There's been a lot of hurt on both sides, so it'll take more time yet, but yesterday at breakfast, he asked if I'd help out at the dealership while Luke's away, so that's... something."

"Is that what you want to do now, work at the dealership? I remember Luke saying something about a business proposal in the car the other night."

Lips lifting in a sardonic smile, Edward said, "Me working at the dealership was always Dad's dream, not mine. Besides, Emily helps him run the place now." He laughed softly. "She says she's revolutionising it. Dad reckons he can't find a damn thing since she took over the office." Then he ducked his head, suddenly shy, afraid Karen would find his ideas frivolous or stupid. "And as for that business proposal, I'm starting my own vintage auto garage."

"You are?" She sat up straighter in his lap and stared at

him with a combination of wonder and awe. "That's brilliant."

Edward smiled at her. What the hell had he been worried about? She was looking at him exactly the same way she always had.

As though she was glad to know him.

Happy to have him in her life.

Worthy of her time.

Worthy of her.

"Tell me more. I want to hear all about it."

But Edward was tired of talking about himself. Besides the day Luke had hired him, when he'd wanted to know everything there was to know about his new chauffeur— warts and all—he couldn't remember the last time he'd been the centre of so much singular attention.

"Another time, baby," he said, nuzzling Karen's cheek. "I'd rather hear all about roller derby, and more to the point, when do I get to see you and your shorty-shorts in action?"

Chapter Ten

Ignoring his request to tell him tales from the track, Karen pressed her lips to Edward's and kissed him slowly, taking his mouth in a leisurely assault until he tightened his hold on her and moaned her name.

"Karen." He nibbled her lips, plucked at them with his own sensuous mouth. "Baby."

He flexed his hips, and she felt the thick length of his erection press against her. She wanted him desperately, wanted to feel him inside her, on top of her. Wanted to feel his heat surrounding her, his breath branding her neck as he whispered all those dirty things he'd promised her. Wanted to see the darkness in his gaze as he took what he wanted from her.

When he shifted her so she straddled him in the chair, her pulse spiked with the realisation that finally, blessedly, Edward *was* taking control.

"Fuck going slow," he growled against her mouth. "I want you, baby. So fucking much."

And she was going to stop him.

She had to.

Edward had been honest with her about his past, and she needed to reciprocate. Before they took this any further, she needed to share with him her darkest hour. Her sob story. Only hers was far more recent.

She needed to tell him about the incident in November.

Pulling away from their kiss, she let her head loll back until she stared at the ceiling, then let loose a sound that was part tearless sob, part tortured chuckle.

"I can't believe I'm about to say this, but we need to put the brakes on for just a little bit longer."

A strangled groan escaped Edward's mouth, and his hands tightened on her arse, pulling her closer so she felt every rock-hard inch of his cock pushing to escape his trousers.

"You sure about that?" he said, his mouth hitched up at one corner, the half grin he threw at her emphasising the same words she'd thrown at him on Saturday night.

It would be so easy to slide his zipper down, to reach inside his briefs and wrap her fingers around his heated length. She wanted to feel the silky skin that enveloped all that strength. Wanted to slide to her knees and take him in her mouth, watch his gaze shutter as he found his pleasure and know she'd been the one to give him that.

But it wouldn't end there.

And what if he did something to trigger her? What if she pushed him away and he didn't know why?

He had to know.

She had to tell him.

Suddenly it all became clear why she'd been trying so hard to jump his bones. It wasn't just her body that craved the reassuring touch of Edward's gentle hands but her mind and spirit too.

And quite possibly her heart.

"I'm sure," she whispered, then flicked her tongue out to moisten her dry lips and took a deep breath. "Do you remember towards the end of last year, when I had those two weeks off?"

"Yes, I remember. Claire said you were sick."

Karen took another breath and slowly let it out. "I was in the hospital for a couple of days, but I wasn't sick."

Edward's jaw tightened, causing the muscle in his cheek to tick. "I'm not going to like this, am I?"

"Probably not, no."

"What happened, baby?" His gaze grew careful. "Whatever it is, you can tell me. I trusted you with my sob story." He stroked gentle fingers down her cheek. "I promise you can trust me with yours."

Tears welled in her eyes again, and she pressed her lips together as tightly as she could in a bid to stem their flow. She'd already blubbered all over the poor bloke once tonight, and she'd never get through this if she dissolved into tears every time he said something kind.

With a nod, she straightened her spine. She could do this. "Okay. Here it is. Three months ago, I attended a house party to celebrate the end of the roller derby competition. All the teams from our league were invited. It wasn't anything formal or even particularly organised, but when these chicks party, it's always a blast. There's dancing and music and swimming and food and—"

She cut herself off as the memories of that night rushed in, reminding her that not all was right with her world. She squirmed in Edward's lap, rolled her shoulders and chewed her lip.

He rubbed his hands up and down her arms, the gesture simple but soothing. "Take your time, Karen. We've got all night."

She took another minute to calm herself, to utilise the mental tricks her therapist had taught her, steps to follow when she felt overwhelmed.

Breathe. Breathe and focus.

And through it all, Edward waited patiently. Just continued offering her silent support by rubbing her arms and occasionally stroking her hair.

When Karen was ready, she continued.

"Our team did well last year, even though we didn't make it to the finals, but we were all in the mood to let loose. I'm not a big drinker at the best of times, but that night I wasn't drinking at all. I was supposed to meet Claire and Lottie for brunch the following morning to discuss wedding plans, so the last thing I needed was a hangover.

"I arrived at the party with one of my teammates and her boyfriend. I didn't usually have much to do with Nathalie Graves. She was...." Karen scrunched up her nose as she searched for the right word.

"What?"

"Peculiar," she said, frowning. "Everyone else on the team thought the sun shone out her arse, and to this day I don't know why. When you really listened to what she said, it was all just empty platitudes and clichéd motivational bullshit. Honestly, it all sounded like it came off a Meme-of-the-Day calendar. And when she wasn't on the track, she dressed like a boho wannabe and stank of cheap coffee and incense.

"But her boyfriend,"—she swallowed hard, then made herself say his name—"Jeremy, had always seemed quite nice, really. Always happy to lend a hand with the equipment, always up for a chat. I didn't know what he saw in her."

"Why did they give you a lift to the party?"

"My car wouldn't start that day, and I didn't have time to fix it. Nathalie lived the closest to my dad's house, so she'd given me a lift to watch the final bout as well as to the party. And as weird as I found her, I had no real reason not to trust her. But not long after we arrived at the party, I began feeling really sleepy, way more than I should have. My head felt fuzzy, as though I'd been drinking all night, but all I'd had was a glass of soft drink."

Edward stopped stroking her arms and tightened his grip, and when he lifted his gaze to hers, Karen saw the darkness she'd seen in him when he'd told her about his past. That shimmer of danger that lurked beneath the surface of his more polished exterior.

The feral animal ready to attack.

Or defend.

"What happened next?"

She snuggled into his chest, and as his arms came around her and held her close, she breathed in his rich scent. A scent so different from that night, warmer, smoother. Comforting.

"I went into the bathroom to splash water on my face, and when I came out, Jeremy was waiting for me."

Tension rippled off Edward, and he held her tighter, then practically snarled, "What did he do?"

"He said Nathalie had sent him to check on me, which I remember thinking was weird because how did she even know I felt sick? I told him I was going home, and that's when he grabbed my arm and started dragging me down the hall. He shoved me into a bedroom." Karen's voice wavered as fresh tears tracked down her cheeks. "I told him I felt sick, that I wanted to go home, but he started trying to undress me, told me to lie down, said he'd make me feel all kinds of better."

Her voice hitched, and she swiped at her tears as she pushed through the horrible memories. "I tried to shove him away, but I felt so weak, like all the strength in my body was just gone. Even my voice felt small. I told him to stop, but he wouldn't leave me alone. And then Nathalie burst into the room and found us together. Jeremy had my shirt and bra off and was lying on top of me, kissing me. I begged her to help me, but she attacked me instead. She punched me and kicked me and there was nothing I could do to stop her. She screamed at me for betraying her, for stealing her boyfriend, then called me a slut and a cunt and told me I'd regret what I'd done."

Karen took a deep breath and slowly pushed it out as she tried to calm herself. Edward kept stroking her hair. "Nathalie's yelling was loud enough to get attention, and I remember other people coming into the room and seeing me like... that. Half naked, bloodied and helpless."

"How did the boyfriend explain himself?" he growled, his voice dark and tight.

"He didn't. He and Nathalie took off." She shook her head. "I'm not sure who helped me after that—it was all kinda blurry—but I remember Eric picked me up from the party and took me to the hospital. They confirmed I had GHB in my system, and also—thank God—that Jeremy hadn't managed much more than getting my top off."

Edward tightened his arms around her to the point that she struggled to breathe. "Tell me that sonofabitch got what was coming to him," he snarled. "Tell me your brothers took care of him."

Karen sniffed loudly and shook her head. "He was arrested, but they had to release him due to a lack of evidence."

"What the fuck?" He pulled back to stare down at her. "Are you fucking kidding me?"

"There were so many people at that party, they couldn't prove Jeremy was the person who spiked my drink, and because no one saw him force me into the room, or heard me tell him 'no', it was his word against mine, and he said it was consensual.

"He told them I was crying because I felt bad about betraying Nathalie, not because he was rough with me. He told them I like it rough." Karen looked away. Her jaw wobbled, and her vision glazed with tears. "He told them that because it's true, but I don't know how he knew that. I never told him that."

Edward gentled his voice. "You're a passionate woman, Karen, open to possibility and honest in your responses. It doesn't take a genius to figure out you'd be that way in bed too." He resumed stroking her hair. "He told them just enough truth to muddy the lie. It's what guys like him do. It's why they get away with it for so long."

"Yeah, well, it sucks arse."

"I know." Her man kissed her forehead. "Have you considered therapy? I know it sounds clichéd, but it really does help."

He said that as though he had first-hand knowledge, which made her want to snuggle closer and breathe in his scent again.

"I go to a group session every Tuesday night."

"That's good," he said, then coaxed her into sitting up again and cupped her cheeks in his warm hands. "Now, tell me how I can help you. What do you need from me, baby?"

Another wave of emotion threatened to drag Karen down and drown her in tears. Would this man ever stop surprising her with his compassion and generosity?

But she supposed after what he'd been through, he'd appreciate the need for such things—probably more than most—and she finally let go of the tension she'd been carrying since she opened the shop that morning and leaned into the heat of Edward's palm.

"This. Exactly this," she said. "I need you to touch me, kiss me, flirt with me. I need you to treat me like a whole woman and not some fragile, broken thing. And I want you to tell me every dirty thing you promised you'd do to me. Every single one."

"Consider it done," he said, a sly grin slowly spreading across his handsome face. "What else?"

"I want to feel you on top of me, inside me," Karen said, mirroring his grin now. "I want to surround myself with you, with everything good and forget everything bad."

Her grin slipped, and she looked up at Edward from under her lashes. "I hate what Jeremy did to me, hate that he made me doubt myself. He made me feel small, made me think maybe I should change who I am to become less of a target, and that just pisses me off, because why should I change?"

She lifted her chin, refused to hide. "Why should I have to make myself fit into someone else's narrow-minded idea of who and what I should be? Fuck that! I may be short, but I'm not small. I want to live large, I want to love big, and I want to crush that arsehole under the magnitude of my epic personality."

Karen huffed out one final breath, then stared at Edward and waited for him to process everything she'd just dumped in his lap.

The last thing she expected to see was lust shining in those dark blue eyes of his. Lust and something akin to... pride?

"You're magnificent," he said, then tugged her down to meet his lips in a slow, drugging kiss that would have made her weak at the knees if she wasn't already sitting down. "How about we skip the restaurant and grab a pizza instead?"

"Netflix and chill?" she said hopefully.

Edward helped her to her feet, then grinned down at her. "Whatever you want, baby."

Chapter Eleven

The fact that Edward wasn't speeding all the way to Karen's house was more a sign of his nervousness than any restraint on his part.

And the fact that he was nervous at all was laughable.

But that's what Karen Walker did to him.

She brought him to his knees with a hopeful smile and a request for pizza and sex. And he honestly couldn't think of a single reason to hold back anymore.

He wanted her.

She wanted him.

Their laundry had been fully aired, and they were still on the same page, plot twists and all, so why the fuck shouldn't they be burning up the sheets?

Karen pulled her car into the driveway first, and Edward parked behind her. Then he followed her across the yard and up her front steps, watching the tantalising sway of her hips as she walked, knowing he'd be gripping them later as he drove himself into her from behind.

Taking her hard and rough.

Rough....

His mouth tightened at the memory of what she'd told him, and he had to flex his hands and shake out his sudden need to punch something. Men like Jeremy should be castrated. At the very least they should be thrown in prison and given a taste of their own medicine. See how they like being trapped in a room with someone determined to take away their power, their choices.

He shoved his hands through his hair. Maybe he should hold back a little, treat the night for what it was—a second date.

Edward knew he was in this relationship for the long haul—there was no rush on his part—but Karen had specifically asked for "Netflix and chill", and he knew her to be intelligent enough to know exactly what she was asking for. Even so, he was prepared for the fact that she might not be as ready as she thought, that he might have to put the brakes on at a moment's notice.

She didn't want him treating her like she was broken, and he wouldn't, but that didn't mean he wouldn't handle her with care.

He'd let her set the pace, let her take control.

He wasn't opposed to be bossed around in bed by a strong woman.

Karen popped the front door open and invited him inside, then kicked it closed behind them. "Pizza should be here soon," she said, throwing him a coy little glance over her shoulder. "I'm going to change into something more"— she wiggled her eyebrows—"comfortable."

Her bedroom was across the hall from the lounge room, and Edward grinned as she disappeared from view. His grin widened when he noticed Karen hadn't shut her door all the way.

Not that he had any intention of entering her bedroom

until invited, but it didn't take him long to figure out she'd left the door ajar on purpose.

Karen teased him with little glimpses of her legs as she unzipped her boots, her arms when she dropped her blouse on the floor. And he had to bite his fist when she slipped her skirt down her legs and bent over at the waist, flashing him with the full force of yet another sexy pair of barely there underwear that lovingly embraced her gorgeous arse.

Edward was about to lose his battle with self-control when a knock on the front door brought him back from the brink.

The pizza had arrived.

Reluctantly, he relinquished his preferred view of Karen's tight little body for that of the delivery guy, paid him, then shut and locked the door. If the universe was kind to him, he'd be staying the night, and he didn't want to lose momentum by having to stop and lock up the damn house later on.

"Pizza's here," he called out as he removed his suit jacket and slung it over the back of the couch. He loosened his tie. "Where's your remote control?"

Edward was about to sit down when Karen appeared in the doorway.

And the air left his lungs in a punch of breath.

"Holy fuck," he murmured, trying to take her all in at once.

He didn't know where to look.

Karen Walker was a dream made real.

A dream that was stalking towards him wearing nothing but a smile.

"Would you mind terribly if we saved the pizza for later?" she said, walking her fingers up his chest.

He swallowed hard. "How much later?"

She wrapped his tie around her fist. "Breakfast?"

"Perfect."

Karen's sexy smile took on a wicked edge, and he quickly found himself being dragged by his tie across the hallway and into her bedroom.

"Strip," she demanded. "Slowly."

Edward smiled as she made herself comfortable on the foot of the bed and crossed one leg over the other. He watched her gaze shutter with pleasure as he slipped the knot of his tie free and slowly pulled it away from his collar, then tossed the imported silk accessory on the bed, knowing it would come in handy later.

Next, he popped open the buttons of his shirt, just as Karen had done the night of the wedding reception. He took his time, popping one free, then the next, and then the next, all while watching her teeth sink into her bottom lip so hard, he was amazed she didn't draw blood.

When he saw her small hands fist in the bedding, he peeled the soft cotton down his arms, discarding the shirt with a flick of his wrist, heedless of where it fell. Then he reached behind him for the collar of his white cotton undershirt and pulled it over his head, knowing the action would hide his body from her until the last minute.

"Oh hell yes," Karen murmured as Edward straightened to his full height, revealing his half-naked body.

"Like what you see, baby?" he said, preening under her unfettered stare.

Sitting on his arse in a car most days had made him more determined to stay fit. And when his workout buddy was Luke fucking Hardcastle, fit was an understatement. That man was a machine.

On the upside, Edward had abs for days and an arse you could bounce a coin on.

Which Karen seemed to appreciate. She followed her vigorous nod with more lip biting and a whimpered "Uh-huh."

Without looking down, he unbuckled his belt and opened his trousers at the same time he toed off his shoes. He could have gone slower, could have given her more of a show, but his cock ached to sink inside his woman, to hear her feminine cries and moans, to feel her wet heat envelop his flesh as he slid deep inside her.

He wanted her.

He *needed* her.

And the frantic lust he saw reflected back at him in her luminous blue eyes told him she needed him too.

Fuck going slow.

His socks and briefs came off just as quickly as his trousers and shoes, and a moment later, Edward had Karen laid out beneath him, listening to her sigh his name as he kissed his way down her graceful neck.

"Edward. More."

"Whatever you want, baby," he breathed against her skin.

He trailed his lips from one earlobe to the other, teasing the sensitive skin along the line of her jaw with feather-light bites and nips. Then he worked his way down her throat, tasting her with open-mouthed kisses, breathing in her feminine scent.

She smelled sweet, like roses and sun-ripened strawberries. And Edward's favourite new thing was nuzzling against her throat and inhaling that sweetness, like a predator scenting his prey.

Only he was the one in danger of being captured.

And he loved it.

Loved....

Lifting his head from the softness of her breasts, he gazed at her lovely face, traced one digit down her cheek and over her lips, grinned when she nipped at his fingertip and slid her tongue out to wrap around it and gently suck, imitating something he hoped would happen sooner rather than later.

"Naughty girl," he whispered, then kissed her deeply again.

Chapter Twelve

Karen slid her fingers through Edward's silky hair as he deepened their kiss. The man was a master kisser, and she was eager to know what other uses he had for his talented tongue.

She didn't have to wait long to find out as he began trai

ling hot, wet kisses up and down her body, all while stroking every inch of her skin with his rough hands and grinding his pelvis against hers.

"Baby," he moaned. "Need to taste you."

"Yes," she whispered. "Please."

Strong hands gripped her legs and pushed them open, but instead of settling his body between them, Edward moved so his head was level with her pussy, and his arms encircled her thighs, holding them wide.

"Mmm," he hummed, the sound pleased. "I like this."

The feel of his fingers stroking the carefully maintained triangle of hair covering her mound made her shiver with anticipation. The touch of his heated tongue against her clit made her nearly jump out of her skin in pleasure.

How long had it been since she'd had sex with another

human being? Six months? More? Certainly not since meeting Edward.

From the moment they'd met, she'd wanted him. And when he'd started chauffeuring Claire around, started spending more and more time in the bookstore, she'd started fantasising about the man in more and more inappropriate ways.

Sex in the tearoom? She'd imagined that.

In the book stacks? That too.

Up against the wall in the office, banging it so hard they'd shake the pushpins loose until all the crap displayed on the wall tumbled down around them? Yeah, she'd rubbed out one or two to that.

Or three.

Or more.

But none of those silly fantasies could compare to the feel of the real deal, of Edward going to town on her clit, the tip of his tongue working the tiny bundle of nerves like a man obsessed. Certainly like a man who knew exactly what he was doing.

Moaning his name, she writhed beneath him, and even the warning little slap of his hand on her inner thigh couldn't make her stop. He was so good, too good, and she was about ready to burst.

"Edward. Tiger. I'm going to come. Oh God... Edward!"

Her body shook and her thighs quivered, and her pussy clenched around the fingers he'd speared into her at the last moment, the ones he now thrust slowly in and out, imitating what they both wanted to happen.

What she needed to happen.

Desperately.

Edward had been so good to her before, so kind as he'd listened to her talk about her ordeal. She'd felt the tension in his body as she'd laid out the details for him. He'd been angry on her behalf, livid that the perpetrator had gotten away with it. But then he'd softened and held her, stroked her hair and soothed her.

Most importantly, he'd believed her.

And unlike some people, he hadn't accused her of seeking attention, hadn't blamed her for what had happened, or insinuated that maybe she'd asked for it. That maybe her lifestyle choices or sexual preferences or the way she dressed had contributed to the situation.

He'd listened to her, comforted her, and now he was touching her. Loving her. Sexing her up in all the right places.

It felt good.

It felt right.

She felt... adored.

The blatant desire she'd seen on Edward's face when she'd walked into the lounge room naked had made her feel lighter than air, as though the massive weight she'd been carrying around since November had dropped away and she could finally stand tall once more.

Well, as much as a short arse like her *could* stand tall.

Edward made her feel desirable again.

Strong again.

Because even though they'd continued to flirt when she'd gone back to work, she knew she'd pulled back a little bit. Knew she wasn't as open as she had been before the incident.

Knew she'd made herself smaller.

"You're so wet, baby," he whispered, still slowly thrusting with his fingers. "Do you want to keep going?"

Locking her gaze with his, Karen nodded.

It was time to live large.

"Yes. Please."

He slipped his fingers out of her pussy and rubbed her wetness over and around her clit, making her groan as he teased the overly sensitive nub of flesh. "It's all right if you change your mind, okay, baby? I need you to know I'm here with you. No matter what. Okay?"

Happiness tugged her mouth into a wide smile, and she reached up to cup Edward's cheeks. "As long as I can see your eyes and hear your voice, I'll be okay. I promise."

He searched her gaze for an eternity, but finally satisfied with what he saw, he left the bed and sheathed himself in a condom. When he came back, he knelt between her spread thighs and slid his hands over her hips, then whispered, "Are you ready?"

"Ready," she whispered back, then pulled him down on top of her.

Edward reached between them and grabbed his cock, lined up their bodies, and slowly slid home.

And it felt... so. Fucking. Good.

His cock was thick and long and filled her up, and her greedy body had taken all of him, swallowed him whole until he bottomed out inside her.

He leaned his forehead against hers and breathed deeply. "You're so tight, baby," he murmured. "But you feel so goddamn good." He started to move, to pull back for another deep thrust. "I could stay inside you forever."

Karen giggled at the thought, then moaned as he continued thrusting, fucking her harder, slamming his cock deeper. "More," she begged. "Harder. Please, tiger. Harder."

But Edward pulled out and got to his knees. "Come here, baby," he demanded, his voice a husky growl. Then he hooked his hands around her thighs and tugged her so her arse pressed against his groin and her legs were flush against his chest.

Slipping his dick back inside her pussy, he banded his arms around her legs—one near her knees, the other closer to her hips—and then he told her to hang on to something.

Karen wasn't sure how Edward was doing what he was doing, but it felt fucking amazing. He was thrusting even deeper than before, harder too, and suddenly she felt the bedhead nudging the back of her skull.

But the only thing she had to hold on to was the bedding.

In another feat of strength and agility she knew she'd never grow tired of, Edward changed their positions again, this time rolling to his back and depositing her on top of him.

"Ride me, baby. Take what you need from me."

"Yes."

Spreading her palms over his well-defined pecs, Karen leaned into his strong body and rode him hard. She loved the feel of him inside her, under her. Loved the tiny bite of pain where his fingernails dug weals in her hips as he thrust up into her, matching her enthusiasm with his own.

She adored the look of utter determination and devotion that filled his gorgeous features, especially his midnight blue eyes. And she could write poetry about the way his biceps flexed and his abs clenched as her body began to quiver and quake around his.

"Edward," she cried. "Oh, God, yes! Yes!"

She threw back her head and screamed her release, and he followed right after, bellowing her name.

Collapsing on top of him, she felt his arms come around her, gentle again after such a show of strength, and he stroked circles on her back. Their bodies heaved as they drew air into their lungs, and for what felt like an eon, all Karen heard was their harsh and harried breaths.

"Water," she gasped eventually as she rolled to Edward's side. "I need water."

A soft chuckle came from the man beside her. "I'll get it," he said. "Back in a sec."

She listened to the creak of the timber floorboards as he left and came back again, minus the condom but carrying the pizza box and a bottle of water, a slice of pepperoni pizza clenched between his teeth.

"What?" he said around the food in his mouth. "I was hungry before we had sex. Now I'm ravenous."

Karen laughed, grabbed the water, and took a drink, and Edward got comfortable on the bed, leaning against the bedhead with his legs stretched out before him.

He patted the empty spot beside him. "Come here."

Crawling over to him, she sat by his side and leaned her head on his shoulder, not really sure what to say.

She'd never suffered post-coital awkwardness before.

Of course, she'd never wanted someone to sleep over before either. And the last time she'd asked him, he'd turned her down flat. But part of living large was taking risks.

And she'd never know if she didn't ask.

"Edward?"

"Mm-hmm?"

She gathered her courage and said in a rush, "Will you stay with me tonight?"

He kissed her forehead, snuggled closer. "There's nowhere I'd rather be."

Chapter Thirteen

Two weeks later, Edward was exhausted.

He'd never had so much sex in all his life.

Karen was insatiable.

And he was head over heels in love.

Hell, he'd already been a little bit in love with her for months. Their flirting sessions at Novelteas, brief as they were, were the highlights of his day. But getting close to her now, getting to know her better, had only deepened his feelings for her.

She was the one.

He knew it as surely as he knew his morning wood wasn't going down any time soon, not without a little human intervention.

Rolling to his side, he coiled his body around Karen, spooning her. "Baby?" he murmured against her shoulder. "You awake?"

She made a non-committal sound that made him chuckle. He had kept her up late.

"Wanna fuck?" he whispered, then ran his tongue around the shell of her ear.

"I'm awake," she breathed sleepily, looking over her shoulder and bending her knee, shifting her leg so Edward could slide two fingers into her from behind. *So wet already?*

"Did you have a dirty dream, baby?" he whispered against her nape, slowly fingering her, stretching her open, making her ready for him.

"Maybe," she whispered back, and he heard the smile in her sultry voice. Then she pushed her arse back and wiggled it against his aching cock. "You wanna hear about it?"

"You know I do."

Edward loved that they'd progressed to a point where Karen felt comfortable being so open with him. Loved that she trusted him, that she felt safe with him. Safe enough to let him fuck her from behind, where she couldn't see his face.

Trusted him enough to let him get a little rough with her, to pull her hair and smack her arse, to bite her and boss her around. To leave his marks on her body.

Grabbing a condom from the bedside table, Edward winced as he rolled it on. His cock was sensitive to touch and his balls felt ready to explode, which meant this was going to be embarrassingly quick. "Tell me about your dream," he murmured against her neck, needing the distraction. "Tell me everything."

Karen moaned as he teased her with his fingers, then said, "We were in the office at the shop and you were fucking me against the wall."

"I like this dream already." He added a third finger to her pussy, making her cry out, making her breath stutter and her breasts heave. "Tell me more."

"You're fucking me against the wall and—oh, God," she

whimpered, then swallowed hard, her body clamping down on his hand. "And the wall shakes every time you thrust into me. Invoices and receipts start falling off the wall, raining down around us."

"Like our very own ticker-tape parade," he said, making her laugh while pressing a smiling kiss to her shoulder.

"Exactly."

"Then what happened?" Edward chose that moment to slip his fingers free of her silken heat, then slide his hand along her thigh, lift her leg a little higher and feed his cock inside her welcoming pussy.

They both groaned as he sank all the way into her, and their conversation was momentarily forgotten.

The feel of her hot core wrapped around his rigid flesh, squeezing him, fucking him as he drove into her again and again was torture. Sweet, rapturous torture. The firm press of Karen's fingers where she reached between her legs and stroked his cock as he slid in and out of her threatened to undo him even sooner, but he was determined to hold out for as long as possible. To make it good for both of them..

"Naughty girl," he whispered against her skin, then grabbed her soft hip in a punishing squeeze and demanded, "Touch yourself. Play with your clit."

"I love it when you talk dirty," Karen said, her voice little more than a whimper, then she did as she was told, bit her lip and groaned again.

Edward grinned as he nibbled and licked and kissed a path along her shoulder, then nuzzled the crook of her neck and inhaled the scent of her skin, breathed in the faint traces of her jasmine soap and let it fuel his lust. "Tell me the rest of your dream."

"Not much to tell," she said between panted breaths. "Wall, fucking, ticker-tape parade, me screaming your name, you shoving me to my knees and coming down my throat." She tried to shrug. "You know, the usual."

Driving into her with one hard thrust, Edward stilled. "Fuck, baby, but you make me want to do so many bad things to you." At the sound of his lover's happy little giggle, he rolled their bodies so Karen was laid out beneath him, then shifted to his knees. Digging his fingers into

her hips, he pulled her up so she was kneeling too, then eased his cock back inside her delicious heat.

Slowly he began thrusting again, taking his time, teasing her, teasing himself. Gripping her arse cheeks in both hands, he pulled the soft globes apart and stroked the pad of his thumb over her arsehole. He smiled at the way her body quivered under the barely there touch, grinned at the sound of her whimper as he gently pushed his thumb inside.

"Edward," she moaned, pushing back harder, pushing both his cock and his thumb deeper. "Please."

"Tell me what you want, baby."

Karen hung her head and groaned, then pushed back again and rotated her hips. Tried using her body to demand satisfaction.

Edward delivered a hard and fast smack on her pert little bum. "Be a good girl for me, Karen. Use your words."

She turned her head to stare at him over her shoulder, the wild look in her eyes screaming what her pretty mouth barely whispered. "Please, fuck me harder. Faster. Please Edward, make me scream."

Keeping his gaze locked to hers, he increased his speed and powered into her. He took her tight body as hard and as fast as he liked, as hard and as fast as he knew *she* liked. Removing his thumb from her arse, he gripped her other hip and hammered into her until her head fell forwards and he felt the telltale flutter of her pussy walls tightening around him.

Karen threw her head back. "More. Please."

He smacked her arse, delivered strike after strike as he plowed into her, delighted in the little sounds she made and the jiggle of her heated flesh. He reached forwards and fisted his hand in her hair, yanked her head back so he could see her face again, see her hooded eyes and parted lips.

"Edward!" She was coming.

And so was he.

"Karen, baby," he gasped, pumping into her twice more before groaning, "Fuck."

He held her like that for a moment, savoured the feel of her heat wrapped around him, the softness of her skin pressed against his, the silkiness of her hair as it fell through his fingers. And when Karen fell forwards onto her stomach again, Edward fell to her side, making sure he didn't crush her under his weight.

"That was... wow." Her voice was muffled by her pillow, but he took the compliment anyway.

"Ditto," he said, and meant it. His orgasm had been such an intense burst of ecstasy, his brain had ceased to form proper sentences. And when Karen rolled to her side and looked up at him, her easy smile and bright eyes stole the rest of his wits.

"I love you," he said, the thought leaving his mouth before it had even fully formed.

But once it was out, he didn't regret saying it. Knew it felt right.

That *they* felt right.

Karen's eyes widened, and he could practically see her mind doing somersaults trying to figure out if he was messing with her or not, and suddenly he wanted to line up every douchebag who'd ever filled her with those doubts and punch them in the throat.

How could anyone make this amazing woman feel less than worthy of all good things?

And if Edward ever met the cocksucker who'd attacked her, he wouldn't hold back. He'd beat the shit out of that motherfucker until he was nothing more than a greasy smear on Edward's fist.

It was the same feeling he'd had when Amber had threatened to let her crew loose on his mother and sister.

No one hurts my family.

And that's what Karen was to him now. Like Luke and Claire, she was family.

His found family.

Although maybe of a different sort.

Her small hand came to rest on his cheek, and one corner of her mouth tipped up in a grin. "We're going to be late," she said, then attacked his mouth with all the passion he'd come to expect from one of her kisses.

He tried not to read anything into the fact that she'd not returned his declaration of love.

He'd known it might take her a little longer to get where he was. He wouldn't begrudge her the time she needed to see he'd never hurt her.

Karen ended their kiss and slid from the bed, and Edward followed her. They had things to do and places to be, namely her dad's house for a family barbeque lunch.

And they were bringing the salad.

Chapter Fourteen

Edward pulled up in front of Karen's childhood home in Beenleigh, south of Brisbane, and killed the engine.

Her brothers were there already, judging by the number of cars parked in the driveway, and he saw her hands clench on the Tupperware container in her hands at the sight of them.

"God only knows what they've told Dad about you, but I'll apologise in advance."

Edward chuckled and rested his hand over hers, gently squeezing her fingers until she released her death grip on the potato salad.

"It's going to be okay, Karen. These things never end up being as scary as you imagine they will be. And hey, on the plus side, you come from a family of cops, so meeting a criminal is nothing out of the ordinary for them."

She almost laughed. "I know you're joking, but wait until you meet him. Dad can be... tough."

"I can deal with tough. And hey, tomorrow you get to meet my dad. We can exchange notes."

She laughed out loud, and the tension eased from her body. She'd been nervous about this meet-and-greet since her father had sent her a text on Wednesday telling her to invite "the convict" over for a "chat".

Edward had a hunch his new nickname wasn't going away any time soon.

They entered the house through the front door, and he quickly found himself in a time warp. The Walker home hadn't been redecorated for at least thirty years.

His mother would be mortified.

Elaine Berringer was a prestigious interior decorator who ran her own business, and Edward could only imagine what the sight of so much off-white and mission-brown would do to the woman's blood pressure.

When they entered the kitchen, two of Karen's brothers were prepping food. One of them he recognised as Eric, but the other was unfamiliar.

"Morning, Kiki," Eric said, then nodded at Edward. "Convict."

Edward tried not to glare at him, then sighed. Like Eric gave a fuck what Edward thought. The arsehole chuckled as he took the container from Karen and put it in the fridge.

"Don't call him that," Karen snarled, then indicated the other man with a wave of her hand. "Edward, this is our younger brother, Tim. Tim, this is my *boyfriend*," she said, emphasising the word as she levelled a firm glare at Eric, "Edward."

Tim's smile was as easy as his sister's. He reached out and shook Edward's hand. "Good to meet you. I've been hearing a lot about you."

"Oh?"

"We pulled your file," Eric admitted, grinning. His smile was nothing like his sibling's. Eric was pure predator.

Like a fucking shark. But then he nodded, the action concil-iatory. "You'll do."

At his words, Edward felt the strain he hadn't known he'd been holding on to leave his body, and Karen gave *his* fingers a squeeze.

"Where's Dad?" Karen asked, shifting gears.

"Firing up the barbie."

"And are we eating inside or out?"

"Outside," Dane said as he pushed his way through the screen door that led to the patio. "Morning, Kiki. Convict."

Karen opened her mouth to protest again—his sweet champion—but Edward just shook his head, resigned to it. "It's okay, baby. Really."

She didn't look convinced, so he leaned down and kissed her again, flipping off her brothers as he did and ignoring the gagging noises they made.

"Barbie's ready."

The deep, bellowing voice could only have come from Karen's dad, and within seconds of the shout, each Walker sibling was trooping out the door to the patio, arms laden with meat and salads.

"Ready to meet the firing squad?" Karen whispered, holding the screen door open so he could walk through unimpeded.

Edward caught her eye and winked. "I don't need to impress him, Karen. Only you."

He knew he'd said the right thing when her smile went all shy and goofy. *This woman.*

Eric introduced Edward to their father, Sam, a retired police sergeant, and was shocked when the arsehole actually used his name. Obviously they'd seen something in his records that assuaged their instincts to be dicks to him, for the most part.

He didn't really care one way or the other as long as they didn't upset Karen anymore.

An interrogation followed in which they asked Edward about his work, his family, and his plans for the future. And he almost burst out laughing at their eagerness to hear more about his plans for a vintage auto garage and his father's collection of restored cars.

"Still don't have a garage though," he admitted. "I want to lock that down before Luke gets back."

"And what's the name of this business going to be?" Sam asked.

"Haven't figured that out yet either. I have a short list of possible names, but I'm not sold on any one of them in particular."

The rest of the day passed pleasantly enough. Food was eaten, beer drunk, and stories shared. Including—to his surprise—what had happened to Karen in November. She'd mentioned roller derby training was starting up again the following week and was worried the attacks on her character—and her car—would start up again.

"What do you mean?" Edward asked. When Karen looked about to shy away from the topic, he squeezed her hand. "You can tell me, baby. You can trust me."

She rewarded him with another small smile, then nodded. "Okay. After I returned to work, I started receiving threatening notes. At first, I found them tucked under the windscreen wipers, but then they started taping them all over my car."

"What did they say?"

"Just stupid stuff like 'we're watching you' and 'watch your back'. And they let the air out of my tyres a couple times. But one night, a few days before Christmas, I went out to my car and found the word... a word spray-painted across the windscreen."

Edward's eyes narrowed, and his voice darkened. "What word?"

"Cunt," Dane said, his tone dripping with disgust.

Cunt. That's what that bitch Nathalie had called her when she'd been attacked. "Why didn't you tell me?" he asked softly, covering her hand with his as he stared at her.

She shrugged and shifted uncomfortably. "I didn't even tell Claire." She scowled and shook her head. "Anyway, it happened months ago."

Eyes still narrowed, he looked to Eric and Dane. "Tell me you did something about this."

"We did," Eric confirmed, his expression grim. "But without actually harming Karen, the most anyone could do was slap the bitch with a restraining order. It seems to have worked though. Haven't heard a peep out of her since."

Edward grunted, his mood soured by the conversation. Then Tim made his excuses and readied to leave, and his family rebounded, all joining in to tease the youngest Walker about how his timing always seemed to coincide with when the dishes needed doing.

"I'm due back on base," he said, throwing his hands in the air as he backed away from his siblings. "Honest, a soldier's work is never done." Then he shook his father's hand, turned towards Edward, and said, "Good to meet you, convict."

Edward chuckled, Karen scowled, and Sam shooed them away when they tried to help clean up.

"We've got this," he said. "Kiki, why don't you show Edward the garage instead?"

"What's in the garage?" he asked, one brow raised.

Their answering chuckles certainly piqued his interest.

Karen grabbed his hand and led him to a large shed at the rear of the yard, then opened the small side door and ushered him inside. With the flick of a switch, the electronic tinkle of fluorescent lights flickered on.

"Ta-da!"

"Damn." Edward stood in awe of a workshop that rivalled his father's for sheer volume of tools, even if it was contained within a much smaller shed, but it was the cherry-red MGA 1500 that sat in the middle of the room that held his attention. "Fuck me, she's a pretty lady."

Karen's smile was broad, and she practically vibrated with excitement. "Dad's always been a tinkerer," she explained, grabbing his hand and dragging him closer to the car. "He loves all vintage cars, but MGs are his favourite. He had a Midget for a few years but traded her for this old girl. He still needs to gussy her up a bit, but she's solid under the bonnet."

Edward wandered slowly around the car, giving her the attention she deserved, before veering off to check out the vintage tools and memorabilia decorating the walls. One portrait in particular made him do a double take.

"Is that the queen?" he asked, squinting at the framed black-and-white photograph of a very young Queen Elizabeth II wearing some sort of military uniform, standing in front of a truck.

"Yep," Karen said. "Dad's a monarchist."

He pointed at the picture. "But why is she dressed like that?"

Karen laughed and shook her head in disbelief. "Didn't you know? Queen Elizabeth trained to be a motor mechanic during the second world war."

"No shit?"

Edward stared at the photograph a little while longer,

his brain churning as he did. He hadn't known that little fact about their queen, but he'd bet a lot of vintage car enthusiasts would.

And that gave him a great idea.

An idea he was about to tell Karen when he noticed her standing beside the car, twirling a set of car keys around her fingers and looking at him like she wanted to eat him up with a spoon.

"Whaddaya reckon? Wanna take her for a spin?" she said, her voice dropping into that husky purr he'd very recently come to love, the one signalling the car wasn't the only thing she wanted to take for a ride. "Maybe go parking and make out for a while?"

Bingo!

His dick hardened instantly, and his lips tugged up at the corners.

"Baby, you totally get me."

Chapter Fifteen

Fifteen minutes later, Karen steered the car down Hart's Road, towards the local quarry.

"Where are you taking me?" Edward asked, watching her with that grin of his that drove her crazy for him.

"Somewhere I can have my wicked way with you," she said, flashing a grin of her own.

"Well, that sounds promising."

Just before they reached the locked gates of the quarry, Karen turned onto the old side road that led up into the hills behind it, but she didn't go far. It too had a gate barring the way, but there was just enough room for her to turn the car around and put it in park.

Where they sat, they couldn't be easily seen from the road. Eucalyptus trees and scrub bordered them on either side, offering them a screen of privacy from prying eyes.

"No one will bother us here," she said, killing the engine.

Edward unbuckled his seat belt. "And how do you know that?"

"Because the quarry is shut on the weekends." She unbuckled her seat belt too and shifted to face Edward, thankful her small size allowed her to move so freely in the compact car. "And because it's too early in the afternoon for the horny teenage brigade."

"I see." He shifted to face her as best he could in the little car and slid his arm along the back of her seat, played with the ends of her hair. "And how did you know to come here specifically?"

The answer forming in her mind made Karen bite her lip to stifle her laughter, but then she screwed up her nose and relented. "It's possible Tim and I followed Eric and Dane when they brought girls here in high school."

His hand tightened on her nape and pulled her closer. His lips flirted with hers as he spoke. "Oh? And you never came here with a boy?"

One shoulder lifted in a half shrug, and she stared up at him through the veil of her lashes. "Maybe once or twice with my boyfriend."

"Yeah?" Edward pressed his mouth to hers in a teasing kiss before pulling back, his gaze hooded and heavy with lust.

"Yeah." She stole another kiss as she reached for his belt buckle. "But he never got what you're gunna get."

"And what's that?"

The purr of his zipper was followed by a soft masculine groan as Karen reached inside his jeans, slipped her hand under the waistband of his briefs, and wrapped it around his hardening shaft. "This."

She leaned down as Edward shifted in his seat, tilting his hips slightly to give her better access to his cock, then wrapped her lips around the tip of him and sucked him down.

"Oh, fuck," he groaned, sliding his hand into her hair, resting it lightly on the back of her head as she bobbed up and down on his dick.

She loved the feel of his silky skin against her tongue, the hardness of the steel beneath it and the way it jerked in her hands. And she adored the guttural moans she drew from deep within him, loved knowing she had the power to make him make those lusty sounds and needy pleas.

"Fuck, baby. Jesus, yes."

She pulled back and slipped her tongue around the head of his cock, teased the sensitive underside until Edward fisted his hand in her hair and yanked her head up.

He took a moment to calm his breathing, then asked, "How good is the handbrake on this thing?"

Karen grinned. "Why?"

"Because I need to be in you, baby, and there's not enough room in here for what I have in mind."

Thankfully the car was parked on relatively flat ground, because what Edward had in mind was to bend her over the curved surface of the boot and slip her panties off. He barely had the condom on before he was fucking her hard and fast, fingering her clit and telling her what a bad girl she was.

And she loved every second of it.

She loved it even more when he dragged her over to the big metal gate behind them and lifted her, wedging her between him and the gate.

"Wrap your legs around me," he demanded, his voice a deep growl. "And hold on tight, because I'm not stopping until you scream my name."

Doing as she was told, her breaths were heavy with lust and wanting, panting out of her like a bitch in heat. "Yes,

Edward," she whispered, staring into his dark blue eyes, desperately wishing he would kiss her.

As he slid back inside her, groaning as he filled her pussy with his delicious cock, her wish was granted. He slammed his mouth against hers and stole her breath.

She whimpered and moaned, their tongues stabbing at each other in a frenzy of need.

Yes.

This was what she wanted.

This was what she *needed*.

Since the first night they'd fucked, Edward had been so careful with her, making sure nothing would trigger her, and she appreciated his consideration more than he would ever know. But she knew him, trusted him, knew he would never do anything to hurt her.

Underneath the roguish persona he projected to the world at large, he was actually quite a sweet man, and one hell of a sensual lover.

To say he'd been generous with the orgasms was an understatement.

But Karen liked her sex rough. She liked it hard and fast and dirty, and as sweet as the sex had been between them at first, she couldn't be happier that Edward had finally let his Dominant side out to play.

The last few days had been wild in bed. And now here they were, fucking up against a metal gate where anyone could happen to pass by and see them.

Excitement lit along her veins, the thrill of it, the possibility of getting caught adding to the magic of his thrusting hips and bruising grip, his fingers digging into her arse as he held her up.

She ran her hands over his biceps, felt the solid mass of

them straining against his T-shirt, the strength of them turning her on even more than she already was.

Fuck.

She wanted to come.

Needed to come.

But she needed some clit action to push her over that line.

Tucking one arm around Edward's neck, she slid her free hand between their bodies and touched herself, circled her finger around the sensitive nub of nerves and flesh, spreading her wetness where she needed it most.

Edward dropped his head back and groaned. "Baby, I love it when you play with yourself. Your pussy tightens around my dick, and it feels so fucking good."

"You like that?" she whispered, her breathing coming in such short, sharp gasps, her voice had all but deserted her.

"You know I do."

"Good, because—" She didn't finish the thought. Her orgasm stole whatever she was going to say and translated it all into one word. "Edward!"

Her lover thrust up into her as she shattered all around him, until he too cried out, yelled her name, and shuddered against her.

They waited until their breathing calmed again before he let her down. Then he helped her step back into her panties and straighten her skirt before taking care of the condom and putting his cock away.

And then he wrapped his arms around her and kissed her cheeks, her jaw, her mouth. Slowly, deeply.

Lovingly.

"I meant what I said this morning, Karen. I love you."

She opened her mouth to respond, but no words came out.

Edward leaned his forehead against hers. "I know you're not there yet, I know you need more time, but I need you to know I'll wait." He pulled back and searched her eyes. "I need you to understand, I'm not going anywhere. I'm here for the long haul. And if you decide this isn't what you want, if you change your mind and only want to... to call me Teddy," he said, the smile he plastered across his face doing nothing to hide the hurt, the longing in his dark eyes, "well, I'm here for that too."

Karen reached up and cupped his cheek, stroked his stubbled jaw. She'd wanted to tell him how she felt that morning when he'd told her he loved her for the first time. She'd wanted to throw her arms around his neck and hold him tight, to never let him go. But she'd held back.

And she'd hurt him.

She'd seen it then, and she saw it now, even as the words sat on the tip of her tongue, desperately wanting to take that leap into the next phase of their relationship, but everything was moving so fast. They'd flirted for five months, dated for two weeks, and now they were making declarations of love?

Sharing her body was one thing. Sharing her heart was another, entirely different thing. She couldn't say it.

It *was* too fast.

Even for her.

But he'd said he'd wait. He'd said he was there for the long haul, that he wanted to be with her, have a future with her.

And that melted her heart even more than those three tiny words.

Edward was right. Karen did need more time, but she knew when the moment was right, she wouldn't hesitate to tell him how she felt.

In the meantime, she leaned in and kissed him. Twisted

her tongue around his and breathed his breath as though it were her own.

She had no idea how long they stayed like that, wrapped around each other, her fingers speared through his short hair, his hands on her arse, holding her close, grinding a fresh erection against her belly.

When they pulled apart again, Edward's eyes had lost their wariness, and his body felt less tense under her hands. "We should probably get back," he said, his grin making a reappearance. "Before your dad thinks I've stolen his car as well as his daughter."

"We wouldn't want that," she agreed, then thumbed over her shoulder at the driver seat. "Wanna drive?"

"I thought you'd never ask." Within a minute, they were buckled in, and the engine roared to life. "Now I'm going to show you what this baby can really do."

Karen's lips quirked as she slid her aviators into place. "Hit it, tiger."

Chapter Sixteen

When Karen and Edward got back to her place, the sun was already setting. The late-summer sky was filled with beautiful orange clouds, tinged with pink and slowly meandering across the sky.

The family barbeque she'd been stressing over had gone off without too many hitches, her brothers and father all seeing for themselves that Edward was a decent man and not some evildoer looking to lure her to the dark side. And their little drive after lunch had given her something else to think about.

What her future with Edward would really look like.

Tomorrow morning, she'd be meeting his family at their weekly Sunday breakfast, and she hoped her introduction went as well as his. He'd assured her his family would adore her, and she found his confidence settled her nerves somewhat.

She trusted him to take care of her.

But as Edward pulled into her driveway, all that stress came roaring back, dragging her old friends fear and loathing with her.

Standing on her veranda was a woman, one she never thought she'd see again.

Karen froze, her eyes locked on the intruder.

"Nathalie."

"What?"

"On the veranda. That's her. That's Nathalie." She'd recognise that thin-lipped, pinch-faced, straw-haired boho-wannabe anywhere. Emphasis on the *ho*.

Sudden panic spiralled through Karen's body, and she broke out in a cold sweat.

What the hell was she doing here?

And what the fuck did she want?

Wasn't it enough that her team had dropped her like a hot potato, believing her to be the boyfriend-stealing slut Nathalie told them she was?

How many times was she going to have to defend herself against this heinous bitch?

How long was this going to continue?

All Karen wanted was to be part of a team, to skate and have some fun. What had she ever done to deserve any of this?

"Stay here," Edward said gravely, then climbed out of the car.

Karen watched, helpless, as her man strode across her yard and confronted the harpy at her front door.

No. Not helpless.

Fuck that.

She wouldn't be cowed by this woman any longer.

Nathalie wanted to see a cunt?

Karen could be a cunt.

Throwing the passenger door open, she exited the car and went to meet her tormentor. "What the fuck do you want?" she demanded, ignoring Edward as he tried to get her to go back to the car.

"You, you fucking slag." Nathalie jabbed a finger in her direction. "I want you to fuck off out of my life for good."

"What the hell are you talking about, you psycho? I want nothing to do with you. I've *had* nothing to do with you for months. Not since your fucking arsehole of a boyfriend put something in my drink and tried to rape me."

"Baby, get back in the car and let me handle this," Edward said, voice stern, one hand held out to try and ward her away, the other pressing his phone to his ear.

But Karen didn't hear what he said next because something in Nathalie's expression warned her who she should be paying attention to, and it wasn't him. When the stupid hag raced down the steps and charged at her, she knew she was right.

"You fucking bitch," Nathalie screamed, fists swinging. "Jeremy left me. Because of you."

"He left because he's a fucking rapist douchebag, you ignorant twat," Karen snapped back, easily dodging the blows aimed at her head. Growing up with three brothers had some advantages after all. Learning how to fight being one of them.

"He wasn't supposed to fuck you. You did something to him, seduced him. You stole him from me."

"I didn't steal shit from you, you crazy bitch. And he's the one who did something to me! He drugged me, Nathalie. The hospital found date rape drugs in my system. And I know *I* didn't fucking take them."

"He didn't give you those drugs." Her opponent spat the words at her. "I did."

"What?" Karen and Edward barked at the same time,

and then Karen added, "And what do mean he wasn't supposed to fuck me?"

Nathalie's eyes grew wide, manic, as she continued trying to land blows on Karen's body. "He wasn't supposed to do that. He was just supposed to make sure you made a fool of yourself in front of everyone. I gave you that shit to put you in your place, you fuckin' goody two shoes. See how *you* like being humiliated."

Karen was so stunned by the horrible woman's admission that she dropped her guard, and Nathalie finally landed a blow. Her head whipped back with the force of the punch as the woman's fist connected with her jaw, but it wasn't enough to do any real damage.

"Fuck," Edward yelled, stepping forwards. He tried to grab Nathalie, but Karen held up her hand to stay him.

"This bitch is mine." She pointed at the crazy woman. "You wanna fight? Let's fight."

Edward folded his arms over his chest in a show of displeasure, but didn't move to interfere again. "This isn't a good idea, Karen."

"Sure it is," she said, sizing up her opponent. "Think of it as hands-on therapy."

But her man was insisting on taking the high road. "Baby, I've called the cops. They're on their way."

Like a cornered animal, panic lit in Nathalie's eyes, making her face look more pinched than usual. She tried to switch their positions, place herself closer to the fence line instead of the house, but Karen wasn't giving her an inch.

"Oh no you don't," she snarled.

No way was she letting this idiot get away again.

Not this time.

Not happening.

"Let's jam."

Karen dodged a wild swing from her ex-teammate and answered it with a blow of her own. A swell of satisfaction flowed through her as her fist connected with Nathalie's nose and hot blood dripped down her face. Her second blow crashed into the awful woman's jaw. "I never did anything to you, Graves. We might not have been friends, but we were teammates. I always had your back on the track. *Always.* So why the fuck did you do this to me?"

"Because you were too good," she screamed, her face blotchy with her rage. "At fucking everything. I was the star of our team until you came along and humiliated me. Pretty little Karen with your speed and agility and your peppy can-do attitude. Ugh! God, you piss me off."

"And that gives you the right to drug me? Gives your boyfriend the right to assault me? You are fucking insane."

"And you're a cunt!"

Nathalie threw another punch, but instead of blocking it, Karen grabbed the silly woman's arm and used her own momentum to throw her to the ground, where she landed on her backside with an angry yelp. She was just getting to her feet again when the police arrived.

Pointing at Karen, she screamed, "She attacked me!"

It certainly looked like she'd been attacked. The strap on her sandal had snapped, her shorts were covered in grass stains, and her tie-dyed T-shirt was dripped with blood from her broken nose.

"What the—"

Karen didn't finish. Edward laid his hand on her shoulder and squeezed. "Shh."

"Did you seriously just shush me?"

He tugged her closer and whispered very deliberately, "Let her dig her own grave."

Two police officers approached, one splitting off to talk

to Nathalie, who immediately went into hysterics, the other coming towards Karen and Edward. "Are you the person who called this in?"

Edward nodded. "Yes, sir. And we have security camera footage of everything that happened here, including that woman violating a restraining order and attacking my girlfriend."

"Is that how you got the bruise on your face?" he asked, flipping open a notepad.

Karen fingered her jaw, winced, and nodded. "Yes."

"Can I see this footage?"

Edward pulled up a camera feed on his phone that showed everything he said it would.

What the hell? How does he know how to access Claire's security cameras?

"We're going to need a copy of that."

"Absolutely."

The police took brief statements and said they'd be in touch, then put Nathalie in handcuffs. But before they could march the crazy bitch out of there, she got in one final barb. "You think you're so great, Walker, but you're no better than anyone."

"I never thought I was," Karen snarled. "But I'm sure as shit better than you."

Edward slid his arm around her waist and pulled her close, pressed a kiss to her temple. Then Karen slumped against him and groaned. She didn't know if she should laugh or cry and ended up doing a lot of both, unleashing the emotional turmoil of the last three months into one big sobbing, snotty mess, ruining another of her boyfriend's shirts.

"Sorry," she mumbled, hiccoughing a laugh through her tears as she tried to wipe away the mess she'd made.

But Edward didn't care. He swung her up in his arms, just like he had at the wedding reception, and carried her inside the house, kicking the door shut behind them.

"How did you know about the cameras?" she asked.

"I installed them for Claire after her aunt lost the plot, just in case she tried causing any more trouble. They're only on the outside of the house though. Nothing indoors. I promise."

Good to know. But then another thought struck her, one she did give voice to. "I'm gunna have to move," she groaned as he deposited her on the kitchen bench. "Did you see the way my neighbours were watching us? Claire's going to kill me. I've become *that* neighbour." She dropped her head into her hands. "What am I going to do?"

Edward grabbed an ice pack from the freezer. "First things first, my million-dollar baby, we need to get some ice on that jaw."

She stared at him through her lashes. "We?"

Her gorgeous man cocked one brow and half grinned as he lifted her chin and lightly pressed the ice pack to the side of her face. "Yes, we. We're a team, aren't we?"

Karen flinched, the shock of the ice sending a shiver down her spine. But then she stared at him, stared into the eyes of the kind, sweet, sexy man determined to take care of her.

Had it truly only been two weeks since they'd started dating?

It felt like forever.

In a good way. A comfortable, easy way. The way friends were comfortable, only better, because Edward and Karen were *not* friends. And she suddenly realised that forever didn't seem very long at all.

She could do forever if she had this man by her side.

Finally giving in to the feelings she'd been shoving down all day, she traced her fingertips over Edward's sensuous mouth and whispered, "I love you."

He kissed her fingertips and winked. "I know."

She grinned and rolled her eyes. *Such a roguish response.* "So... what would you like to do tonight?" she asked, trying—and failing—to not sound too suggestive.

But apparently she wasn't the only one with a one-track mind, because his answer was perfect.

"Netflix and chill?" he said, his half grin blooming into a wide smile.

Karen laughed, her pain momentarily forgotten as her whole body shook with joy, and she hooked her hand around his neck and pulled him closer. Close enough to feel the heat of his lips only a hair's breadth away from her own when she whispered, "Now that sounds like a plan."

Epilogue

A week later, the swelling had gone down on Karen's jaw, and the bruise had turned from an angry purple to a middling yellow. It was still tender to the touch but far better than before.

"You sure you're feeling up to this, baby?"

This was the first night of the roller derby season. An exhibition bout and recruiting drive for fresh meat to fill out the team rosters.

She hadn't planned on skating. Hell, she'd even considered—for an extremely brief moment of time—not returning to the sport at all. Then out of the blue, she'd received a call from Araminta "Minty" Kapoor, captain of the B52 Bombshells. She'd informed Karen that due to behaviour unbecoming, and the fact that she'd been charged with the crime of administering an intoxicating substance with intent to harm, Nathalie "Graves Digger" Graves had earned herself a lifetime ban from the league.

And then she'd asked Karen to join her team.

It'd taken her a whole five seconds to say yes, firstly because the thought of never seeing Nathalie again was too

134

good an opportunity to pass up, and secondly, the possibility that she'd never actually get on the track again made her heart hurt.

She tugged on Edward's hand and pulled him to a standstill, then slid her arms around his waist. Grinning up at him, she shook her head at the concern etched across his brow. "Stop worrying, tiger. I'm healing just fine. Honestly, I've had worse."

He didn't look convinced, but if he thought scowling at her and scolding her were going to change her mind about strapping on her skates and beating her former teammates to a pulp, he was going to be sorely disappointed.

"That is not reassuring. I don't want to see you get hurt again," he said, leaning his forehead against hers.

Her man was such a softy. "Then you probably shouldn't have insisted on watching the bout." Edward stiffened in her arms. "I am going to get more bruises, and probably a few more scrapes—possibly even a broken bone every now and then—and that's just par for the course on the track." Her grin grew feral. "But I'm also gunna make them hurt. And I'm going to enjoy every fucking second of it."

His scowl and worry were replaced by a grin of his own. "For such a good girl, you're a fucking savage."

"And don't you forget it."

She reached up on her tiptoes and pressed a firm kiss to his delectable mouth. Within seconds his arms had tightened around her, and she felt the press of his hardening cock against her belly.

"For fuck's sake, convict, do you have to maul our sister in public?"

They broke the kiss, and Edward threw her brothers a bemused look. "What are you going to do, Eric? Arrest me?"

"And stop calling him 'convict', please," Karen added as her eldest brother flipped Edward off.

"Well, I'm not fucking calling him 'tiger'."

"Come on, people. Let's go." Dane clapped his hands to hurry them along. "There's hot chicks in shorty-shorts awaitin'."

Tim rolled his eyes and slowly shook his head. "You do know our sister is one of those chicks, right?"

Dane shuddered, then glared at their younger brother. "Why are you like this?"

Inside the arena, Edward's siblings were already seated and waiting. Edward and Karen had forgone the Sunday breakfast meet-and-greet at the Berringers' house due to Karen's swollen jaw but were back on track for the next one.

However, when Edward's sister had discovered Karen was into roller derby, she'd insisted on coming along to watch the exhibition bout, and a more informal introduction of everyone's siblings was arranged.

Emily waved them over. "We saved you some seats."

Two of her brothers pulled up short when they saw the pretty brunette. "Whoa, who's the hottie?" Dane said. "And more importantly, is she single?"

Eric pushed Dane out of his way. "Dibs."

Edward was in his face in an instant. "You even think about touching my baby sister and I will end you."

Broad smirks stretched across her brothers' faces, and Eric and Dane exchanged a look that said no good about to come of this. Then they muscled their way past Edward to join his sister, boxing her in on either side.

Tim shook his head at their brothers, his shoulders bouncing with laughter. "Thank Christ I'm gay," he said, then winked at Karen. "I don't have to compete with those idiots."

Karen snickered, then clapped him on the shoulder and joined the others.

After introductions were made, she left everyone to get settled in their seats and continued across the arena to where her new team was waiting for her.

"How ya' feeling, blondie?" Minty said, greeting her with a wide smile and a high five. "Ready to wipe the floor with those losers?"

"Abso-fucking-lutely," she said, grinning. "Let's take these bitches down."

With the team geared up, Minty called everyone into a huddle. "All right, ladies, it's our first bout of the season, and we're up against a tough crew. And as tempting as it may be to drop these bitches with a well-timed cunt-punch, we're going to play by the rules and beat them as God intended: with inside intel. Karen?"

Karen ran everyone through a quick list of the Deathly Dolls' weak points, game strategies, and dirty tricks to watch out for.

Her former teammates had been glaring daggers at her from the moment they saw her arrive, but she no longer cared. They'd sided with Nathalie over this whole stupid imaginary rivalry bullshit, so presumably they also thought Karen was a stuck-up goody two shoes who deserved to be humiliated.

Well, she was done with other people's opinions.

She was pissed off and ready for payback.

"They'll be gunning for you," Minty warned, handing her the star cap.

Karen pulled the cap over her helmet and flashed her new captain a savage grin. "They can try."

It was time she taught them a thing or two about humiliation.

Edward watched from the edge of his seat as the bout began, his palms sweaty and his heart beating a mile a minute as he watched the opposing team try to crush his woman.

"Fuck, she's fast," Easton said from beside him. "And *really* hot."

"That's my future wife you're talking about, mate. Have some respect."

He couldn't argue though. Karen was *really* hot. He'd only gotten a glimpse of her outfit before they'd left the house, but it'd been enough to give him a hard-on that still hadn't gone all the way down. Now she was speeding around a flat track wearing pink fishnets, black shorty-shorts, and a pink T-shirt with the number 11 and her name in big black letters on the back.

"The Kraken".

Pink skates and helmet, and black knee, wrist, and elbow pads completed the outfit.

Even covered in safety gear, Karen was the sexiest woman he'd ever known.

And she's all mine.

His brother slowly turned to face him. "Future what now?"

Edward refused to take his eyes off Karen. "You heard me, you little shit."

It wouldn't happen any time soon—they'd only been dating for three weeks—but it would happen. He knew it as surely as he knew how to drive a car. And it wasn't just the sex, although that was pretty fucking phenomenal.

Karen just *got* him.

She understood him in a way no girl ever had before.

Sure, they had shared interests, similar tastes in books and movies and music, but she also understood what mattered to him on a fundamental level. She understood his need to succeed at something he was truly passionate about, and she was willing to help him in any way she could.

She had his back.

Karen had even helped him decide on a name for his business when she'd told him about the photograph in her father's garage.

Good Queen Bessie's Vintage Auto Repairs, with the option to add *and Rentals* on the end if he decided to expand in that direction.

Edward's hands tightened into fists as he watched Karen, his blood boiling as he saw a woman on the opposing team try to slam into his girl from the side.

"Emily," he said, reaching over Dane to grab his sister, "what are the rules? Are they allowed to shove Karen like that?"

But it was Dane who answered him. "Aw, don't worry, convict. Kiki can hold her own." Then the smug bastard folded his thick arms across his chest and winked at Emily. And if he hadn't been so worried about Karen, Edward would have knocked his fucking lights out.

"It's called blocking, and yes, they can. They're trying to box her in so she can't score," Emily said as she swapped seats with Easton, earning her protests from both Dane and Eric. "Each member she passes from the other team earns her team one point."

"But if she's stuck in the middle...."

"She can't score," she confirmed. "Oh! But look. See?"

Edward watched, excitement flooding his entire body with adrenaline and endorphins as Karen's team rallied around her and knocked their opponents out of her way, allowing her to score.

The scuffles, or "jams" as Emily called them, went on and on, one after another. He found it all a little confusing. Sometimes Karen wore the star on her helmet, other times not, and he wasn't sure which was more frightening. Edward had seen Karen throw a punch. He knew she could fight. Not that she was throwing punches out there on the track, but he'd never seen her as vicious as she was down there, carving a path for her teammates to follow.

But that was what Karen did.

She took care of the needs of others, whether it be making someone a cup of tea, recommending a book, or taking a job promotion she wasn't sure she was ready for because her best friend was pregnant.

Or helping an ex-con get his life back on track.

She was the type of woman who never asked for anything in return but deserved every good thing the world had to offer. She was the woman he wanted to spend his life with.

His woman.

The woman he'd spend his life making sure he took care of, making sure her needs were met. Whether it be making her a cup of tea, giving her space to read a book, or, when she was ready, getting her pregnant.

She was the one he'd love with all his heart.

A sudden shout from the crowd and a whistle blowing indicated the bout was over, and Edward went in search of his girl.

"I'm not really sure who won," he admitted when she skated into him with a soft bump and wrapped her arms around his waist, her helmet dangling from her hand. "I was a little distracted by the view."

"We won." Karen laughed. "We kicked arse."

His woman was sweaty and smiling, her face red from exertion and her eyes bright and happy.

He wanted to make her look that way for a whole other reason, but taking care of her came first.

Smoothing her damp hair away from her face, he leaned down and kissed her, slowly, passionately. "You're amazing, baby."

"I know," she said with a sly grin.

He grinned back. "You hungry?"

"Famished."

"Then what would you say to some late-night burgers and milkshakes with our siblings?"

"I'd say that's why I love you, tiger."

Edward cocked one brow and tugged her closer, slid his hands down her back until he was cupping her sweet arse. "Oh?"

Karen snuggled closer, let her lips hover over his and whispered, "You totally get me."

I hope you enjoyed Karen and Edward's story.

Please consider sharing the love by leaving a review
for other readers to find. It doesn't need to be
very long, and every review is greatly appreciated.

#sharethelove

Ready for more sexy bachelors?

The Boss Babe CEO and The Scoundrel is next!

Kit Bellows is known for three things: his extreme height, his excellent wine, and for being a cantankerous arsehole. Seriously, the man should come with a warning label.

When tragedy strikes and Kit discovers the family vineyard has been left to Lottie Cassidy—his late cousin's ex-girlfriend—his mood doesn't improve. But if this billionaire bimbo thinks she can just waltz onto his farm and start barking orders at him, she can think again. He doesn't care how smart she thinks she is, and he absolutely doesn't care how goddamn sexy she is. She doesn't belong.

Determined to prove his point, Kit makes Lottie a deal: if she can get through harvest season without breaking a nail, he'll concede defeat, but if she quits, he gets the farm.

The more he pushes her, the more stubborn she becomes, and the more she pushes back, the more he wants to... *kiss* her? But that can't be right. He loathes her. Doesn't he?

More from Jennie Kew

Acknowledgements

To my family for all their encouragement, their love and understanding, thank you for being you and for putting up with me being me, especially when deadlines are involved.

A special thank you to my crit partners, my cheer squad, my sisters-in-arms, Bec McMaster and Kylie Griffin. You always challenge me to be a better writer and I really couldn't do this without you. Thank you for keeping me sane...*ish*.

To my editor, Kristin Scearce, who accepts my weird writing style and quirky humour as canon and is still willing to work with me, you rock!

And finally to my readers, thank you for taking this journey with me, and for allowing me to share with you all the people and places who occupy my head and my heart. I hope you enjoy reading about them as much as I enjoy writing about them.

Meet the Author

Jennie has always enjoyed reading but never had aspirations of becoming a published author. At least not until a dance with death made her ask herself what she really wanted out of life, and she's been writing ever since.

When not writing stories about her imaginary friends, Jennie can usually be found reading a book, watching a movie or building stuff out of Lego. She lives in regional New South Wales with her husband, her husband's magnificent beard, and their small menagerie of furry companions.

www.jenniekew.com

Glossary

As all of my books are set in Australia and use a lot of Australian terms and slang, I've created this guide for my readers to keep you on track when you come across any Aussie-isms in my books.

A bit of all right: If someone is 'a bit of all right' they're considered to be very attractive.

Ambo: Short for ambulance, the term has come to mean anyone associated with any of the public or private ambulance services, their drivers and paramedics.

Arse: Aussie spelling of ass, aka buttocks, bottom, booty and bum.

Arvo and *Sarvo*: 'Afternoon' and 'this afternoon'.

Copper: Police, cops.

Fashion Rag/Local Rag: Fashion magazine, any locally produced magazines or newspapers.

Fierie/s: Firefighter/s.

Fuck-knuckle: An idiot.

G'day: Pronounced 'gidday', this official Australian greeting is a contraction of the words 'good' and 'day'.

Kiwi: Pronounced 'kee-wee', anyone born in New Zealand.

Larrikin: An unruly, boisterous but generally good natured person, usually male.

Mate: Unlike paranormal or sci-fi erotic romances where your 'mate' is the person you're fated to be with for the rest of your life, in Australian culture 'mate' could mean anyone from your best friend to some random bloke you just met.

Pav: Pavlova, a dessert made from baked meringue, topped with cream and fresh fruit, particularly popular around Christmas. We nicked it from the Kiwis.

Phwoar: An estimation of the sound one makes when a bit of all right enters your vicinity. See also, 'panting' and 'drooling'.

RFS: Rural Fire Service.

Sanga: Sandwich.

She'll be right, mate: Usually given as a response when someone is offering aid of some kind, it means 'Everything will be fine but thanks for asking'.

Togs: A swimsuit.

Tradie: Any tradesman.

Uni: Pronounced 'you-nee', University aka College.

Yeah, nah and *Nah, yeah*: Whichever word the phrase ends on, is the affirmative answer, therefore 'Yeah, nah' means 'No', and 'Nah, yeah' means 'Yes'.